Publisher:

FORTUNA PUBLICATIONS

www.fortunapublications.com

Editor:
Michael P. Roberts

Artistic Director:
Beverly A. Harris

----

e-mail address:
fortunapublications@gmail.com

We are soliciting for new stories and artwork to be featured in this magazine. If you have something for us to read or art to show, let us know by email.

EDITORIAL

Welcome to the second issue of **SCIENCE FICTION ADVENTURES**.

We will be presenting a wide variety of science fiction adventure stories from a variety of authors, new and old. If you have a story for us, please let us know.

We hope you enjoy this issue.

I0638021

FUTURE OF SCIENCE FICTION ADVENTURES

Stories scheduled for upcoming issues include:

The conclusion of the **Treasures of Tantalus** serial by Garret Smith
The third chapter in the **Cosmos** round-robin serial
and other old and new stories

Treasures of Tantalus was first published in 1920.
Cosmos, round-robin serial was published in 1933-1934.
Newscast was first published in 1939.
Invisible was first published in 1938.
The Island of Unreason was first published in 1933.

isbn 978-1647200718

The Fiction House Press Replica Line is available at
www.FictionHousePress.com

SCIENCE FICTION ADVENTURES

CONTENTS

April 2020   Vol. 1, No. 2

Front Cover Illustration by Frank R. Paul

THE ISLAND OF UNREASON

By Edmond Hamilton

THE Director of City 72, North American Division 16, looked up enquiringly from his desk at his assistant.

"The next case is Allan Mann, Serial Number 2473R6," said the First Assistant Director. "The charge is breach of reason."

"The prisoner is ready?" asked the Director, and when his subordinate nodded he ordered, "Send him in."

The First Assistant Director went out and re-entered in a moment, followed by two guards who had the prisoner between them. He was a young man dressed in the regulation sleeveless white shirt and white shorts, with the blue square of the Mechanical Department on his shoulder.

He looked a little uncertainly around the big office, at the keyboards of the big calculating and predicting machines, at the televisor disks through which could be seen cities half around the world, and at the broad windows that looked out across the huge cubical metal buildings of City 72.

The Director read from a sheet on his desk. "Allan Mann, Serial Number 2473R6, was apprehended two days ago on a charge of breach of reason.

"The specific charge is that Allan Mann, who had been working two years on development of a new atomic motor, refused to turn over his work to Michael Russ, Serial Number 1877R6, when ordered to do so by a superior. He could give no reasonable cause for his refusal but stated only that he had developed the new motor for two years and wanted to finish it himself. As this was a plain breach of reason, officers were called."

The Director looked up at the prisoner. "Have you any defense, Allan Mann?"

The young man flushed. "No, sir, I have not. I wish only to say that I realize now I was wrong."

"Why did you rebel against your superior's order? Did he not tell you that Michael Russ was better fitted than you to finish development of your motor?"

"He did, yes," Allan Mann answered. "But I had worked on the motor so long I wanted very much to finish it myself, even though it took longer—I realize it was unreasonable of me—"

The Director laid down the sheet

"We came to get you and found you had been having trouble with the other Unreasonables. But we picked you up."

and bent earnestly forward. "You are right, Allan Mann, it was unreasonable of you. It was a breach of reason and as such, it was a blow at the very foundation of our modern world-civilization!"

He raised a lean finger in emphasis. "What is it, Allan Mann, that has built up the present world-state out of a mass of warring nations? What has eliminated conflict, fear, poverty, hardship from the world? What but reason?

"Reason has raised man from the beast-like level he formerly occupied to his present status. Why, in the old days of unreason the very ground on which this city now stands was occupied by a city called New York where men struggled and strove with each other blindly and without cooperation and with infinite waste and toil.

"All that has been changed by reason. The old emotions which twisted and warped men's minds have been overruled and we listen now only to the calm dictates of reason. Reason has brought us up from the barbarism of the twentieth century and to commit a breach of reason has become a serious crime. For it is a crime that aims directly at the demolition of our world-order."

Beneath the Director's calm statement, Allan Mann wilted. "I realize that that is so, sir," he said. "It is my hope that my breach of reason will be regarded only as a temporary aberration."

"I do so regard it," the Director said. "I am sure that by now you realize the wrongness of unreasonable conduct.

"But," he continued, "this explanation of your act does not excuse it. The fact remains that you have committed a breach of reason and that you must be corrected in the way specified by law."

"What is this way of correction?" asked Allan Mann.

The Director considered him. "You are not the first one to commit a breach of reason, Allan Mann. In the past more than one person has let irrational emotions sway him.

These atavistic returns to unreason are becoming rarer but they still occur.

"Long ago we devised a plan for the correction of these *unreasonables*, as we call them. We do not punish them, of course, for to inflict punishment on anyone for wrongdoing would be itself unreasonable. We try instead to cure them. We send them to what we call the island of unreason.

"That is a small island a few hundred miles out at sea from this coast. There are taken all the unreasonables and there they are left. There is no form of government on the island and only unreasonables live there. They are not given any of the comforts of life which human reason has devised but instead must live there as best they may in primitive fashion.

"If they fight or attack each other, it is nothing to us.

"If they steal from each other, we care not. For living like that, in a place where there is no rule of reason, they soon come to see what society would be like without reason. They see and never forget and most of them when their sentence is finished and they are brought back are only too glad for the rest of their lives to live in reasonable fashion. Though a few incorrigible unreasonables must stay on the island all their lives.

"It is to this island that all guilty of breach of reason must be sent. And so as provided by law, I must sentence you to go there."

"To the island of unreason?" Allan Mann said, dismay plain on his face. "But for how long?"

"We never tell those sent there how long their sentence is to be," the Director told him. "We want them to feel that they have a lifetime ahead of them on the island and this brings the lesson further home to them. When your sentence is finished, the guard-flier that takes you there will go there to bring you back."

He stood up. "Have you any complaint to make against this sentence?"

Allan Mann was silent, then spoke in subdued voice. "No, sir, it is but reasonable that I be corrected according to custom."

The Director smiled. "I am glad to see that you are already recovering. When your sentence has expired I hope to see you completely cured."

THE guard-flier split the air like a slim metal torpedo as it hurtled eastward over the gray ocean. Long minutes before the coastline had faded from sight behind, and now beneath the noonday sun there extended to the horizons only the gray wastes of the empty ocean.

Allan Mann regarded it from the flier's window with deepening dismay. Reared in the great cities like every other member of civilized humanity, he had an inborn dislike of this solitude. He sought to evade it temporarily by conversing with the two guards who, with a pilot,

were the flier's other occupants. But Allan found that they disliked to talk much to unreasonables.

"It'll be in sight in a few minutes," one of them said in answer to his question. "Soon enough for you, I guess."

"Where do you land me there?" Allan asked. "There's some kind of city there?"

"A city on the island of unreason?" The guard shook his head. "Of course not. Those unreasonables couldn't cooperate long enough on anything to build any kind of a city."

"But there's some sort of a place for us to live, isn't there?" asked Allan Mann anxiously.

"No place but what you find for yourself," said the guard unsympathetically. "Some of the unreasonables do have a kind of village of huts but some of them just run wild."

"But even those must sleep and eat *somewhere*," insisted Allan with all the firm faith of his kind in the omnipresence of bed and food and hygienic amusements provided by a paternal government.

"They sleep in the best places they can find, I suppose," said the guard. "They eat fruits and berries and kill small animals and eat them—"

"Eat animals?" Allan Mann, of the world's fiftieth generation of vegetarians, was so shocked by the revolting thought that he sat silent until the pilot droned over his shoulder, "Island ahead!"

He looked anxiously down with the guards as the flier circled and came back and dropped in a spiral toward the island.

It was not a large island, just an oblong bit of land that lay on the great ocean like a sleeping sea-monster. Dense green forest covered its low hills and shallow ravines and extended down to the shelving sandy beaches.

TO Allan Mann it looked savage, wild, forbidding.

He could see smoke rising in several thin curls from the island's western end but this evidence of man's presence repelled rather than reassurred him. Those smokes came from crude fires where men were perhaps scorching and eating the flesh of lately-living things

The guard-flier dipped lower, shot along the beach and came to rest with its vertical air-jets spurning up sand.

"Out with you," said the chief guard as he opened the door. "Can stay here but a moment."

Allan Mann, stepping down onto the hot sand, clung to the flier's door as a last link to civilization. "You'll come back for me when my sentence is up?" he cried. "You'll know where to find me?"

"We'll find you if you're on the island but don't worry about that—maybe your sentence was life," grinned the chief guard. "If it wasn't, we'll get you unless some unreasonable has killed you."

"Killed me?" said Allan, aghast.

"Do you mean to say that they kill each other?"

"They do, and with pleasure," said the guard. "Better get off this beach before you're seen. Remember, you're not living with reasonable people now!"

With the slam of its door the guard-flier's jets roared and it shot upward. Allan Mann watched stupefiedly as it rose, circled in the sunshine like a gleaming gull, and then headed back westward. Sickly, he watched it vanish, westward toward the land where people were reasonable and life went safely and smoothly without the dangers that threatened him here.

With a start Allan Mann realized that he was increasing his danger by remaining out on the open beach where he might easily be seen by anyone in the woods. He could not yet conceive why any of the unreasonables might want to kill him but he feared the worst. Allan Mann started on a run up the beach toward the woods.

His feet slipped in the hot sands and though Allan was physically perfect like all other citizens of the modern world, he found progress difficult. Each moment he expected to see a horde of yelling unreasonables appear along the beach. He quite forgot that he was a condemned unreasonable himself, and saw himself as a lone representative of civilization marooned on this savage island.

He reached the woods and plumped down behind a bush, panting for breath and looking this way and that. The forest was very hot and silent, a place of green gloom pillared by bars of golden sunlight that struck down through chinks in the leafy canopy above. Allan heard birds chittering around him.

He considered his predicament. He must live on this island for an unguessable length of time. It might be a month, a year, even many years. He saw now how true was the fact that the prisoner's ignorance of his sentence's length made it all the more felt. Why, he might, as the guard had said, have to spend all his life on the island!

He tried to tell himself that this was improbable and that his sentence could not be so severe. But no matter what its length, he must prepare to live here. The essentials were shelter and food, and escape from the other unreasonables. He decided that he would first find some secluded spot for a shelter, construct one, and then try to find berries or fruits such as the guard had mentioned. Meat was not to be thought of without revulsion.

Cautiously Allan Mann got to his feet and looked about. The green forest seemed still and peaceful but he peopled it with a myriad dangers. From behind every bush menacing eyes might be spying on him. Nevertheless, he must win to a more hidden spot and so he started in through the woods, determining to keep away from the island's western end where he had seen the smokes.

Allan Mann had gone but a dozen fearful steps when he stopped short, whirled. Through the brush someone was crashing toward him.

His panic-stricken mind had not the time to think of flight before the running figure emerged from the brush beside him, then at sight of him recoiled.

It was a girl clad in a stained, ragged tunic. Her limbs showed brown below its tattered hem, her black hair was cut very short, and as she threw herself back from him in alarm a short spear in her right hand flashed up ready to dart toward him.

Had he made a move toward her the spear would have been driven at him; but he stood as quivering and startled as she. Gradually as they confronted each other, the fact that he was harmless became apparent to the girl and some of the terror left her eyes.

Yet with her gaze still upon him she backed cautiously away until just behind her were some dense bushes. With a quick escape thus assured her, she surveyed him.

"You're new?" she said. "I saw the flier come."

"New?" said Allan mystified.

"New to the island, I mean," she said quickly. "They just left you, didn't they?"

Allan nodded. He was still trembling slightly. "Yes, they just left me. It was breach of reason—"

"Of course," she said. "That's what we're all here for, we unreasonables. Those old fogies of directors send someone here every few days or so."

At this heretical description of the executives of the reasonable world, Allan Mann stared. "Why shouldn't they send them?" he demanded. "It's only fair they should correct unreasonables."

Her bright black eyes widened. "You don't talk like an unreasonable," she accused.

"I should hope not," he returned. "I committed a breach of reason but I realize it and I'm sorry I did it."

"Oh," she said, and seemed disappointed. "What's your name? Mine's Lita."

"Mine is Allan Mann. My serial number—" He stopped.

CHAPTER II
First Struggles

A BIRD had called loudly back in the woods and the sound had seemed to recall something to the girl and bring fear back into her eyes.

"We'd better get out of here," she said quickly. "Hara will be along here after me—he was chasing me."

"Chasing you?" Allan remembered with a cold feeling the guard's warning. "Who is Hara?"

"Hara's boss of the island—he's a lifer they just brought a few weeks ago but he's beaten all the strong-est men here."

"You mean that they *fight* here to see who is to be the leader?" Allan asked incredulously. Lita nodded.

"Of course they do. This isn't back in civilization where the best mind ranks highest, you know. And Hara's after me."

"He wants to kill you?"

"Of course not! He wants me for his woman and I won't consent. I never will, either." The black eyes flashed.

Allan Mann felt that he had strayed into some mystifying new world. "His woman?" he said with knitted brows.

Lita nodded impatiently. "When people here mate there's no Eugenic Board to assign them to each other so they simply fight for mates.

"Hara has been after me and I won't have him. He got angry today and said he'd make me but I fled the village and when he and some of the others started after me I was— *listen!*"

Lita stopped with the tense command and Allan, listening with her, heard from somewhere in the woods distant trampling and crashing, a hoarse voice calling and others answering.

"They're coming!" Lita cried. "Come on, quick!"

"But they can't—" Allan started vainly to say, and then was cut off as he found himself running with the girl through the woods.

Branches tore at his shorts and briars pricked his legs savagely as they forced through the brush. Lita led inward toward the island's center and Allan struggled to keep beside her.

His muscles were in the pink of condition but he now found that running from danger through a forest was oddly different from running beneath the sunlamps of one of the great city gymnasiums. There was a tightness across his chest, a cold at his spine, as he heard the hoarse voices behind.

Lita looked back, her face white through its brown, as she and Allan ran. Allan Mann told himself that there was no reason why he should follow this girl into trouble. Before he could formulate the thought further they emerged into a small clearing just as from one side of it there crashed another man.

A bull-like roar of triumph went up and Allan Mann saw that the man was a barrel-bodied, stocky individual with flaming red hair on his head and chest, his hard face alight. He grasped Lita'a arm as the girl swiftly shrank back beside Allan.

"Hara!" she panted, trying in vain to break free.

"Ran away, eh?" he said savagely, and then his eyes took in Allan Mann. "And with this white-faced sheep!"

"Well, we'll see whether he's good enough to take a girl away from Hara!" he added. "You've no spear or club so we'll make it fists!"

He tossed his own club and spear to the ground and advanced with balled fists on Allan. "What do you mean?" asked Allan dazedly.

"Fight, of course!" bellowed Hara. "You wanted this girl and you can fight me for her!"

Allan Mann thought swiftly. Against this brutal fighter he would have small chance—now, if ever, he must use the reason that is man's advantage over the brute. "But I don't want her!" he said. "I don't want to fight for her!"

Hara stopped in sheer surprise and Allan saw Lita's dark eyes stare at him. "Don't want to fight?" cried the other. "Then run, rat!" And as he snarled that in contempt he turned to grasp the girl.

As he turned Allan stooped swiftly, scooped up his heavy club and slammed it against the back of Hara's neck. The red-head went down like a sack of meal.

"Come on!" cried Allan tensely to Lita. "Before he comes to we can get away—quick!"

They rushed in to the brush. Soon they heard the calling voices become suddenly noisy, then die away. They stopped, panting.

"That was brain-work," said Allan Mann exultantly. "He won't come to for an hour."

Lita looked scornfully at him. "That wasn't fair fighting," she accused.

Allan Mann was aghast. "Fair fighting?" he repeated. "But surely when you wanted to get away from him—you didn't expect me to fight him with my fists—"

"It wasn't fair," she repeated. "You hit him when he wasn't looking and that's cowardly."

If Allan Mann had not been super-civilized he would have sworn.

"But what's wrong about it?" he asked bewilderedly. "Surely it's only reasonable for me to use cunning against his strength?"

"We don't care much on this island about being reasonable—you ought to know that," she told him. "But we do believe in fighting fair."

"In that case you can get away from him the next time yourself," he said furiously. "You unreasonables—"

A thought struck him. "How did you come to be sent to this island anyway?"

Lita smiled. "I'm a lifer. So are Hara and most of the others at the village."

"A lifer? What did you do to get a life-sentence in this horrible place?"

"Well, six months ago the Eugenic Board in my city assigned me a mate. I refused to have him. The Board had me charged with breach of reason and when I persisted in my refusal I was sentenced here for life."

"No wonder," breathed Allan Mann. "To refuse the mate the Board assigned—I never heard of such a thing! Why did you do it?"

"I didn't like the way he looked at me," said Lita, as though that explained everything.

Allan Mann shook his head helplessly. He could not understand the thought-processes of these unreasonables.

"We'd better get on into the island," Lita was saying. "Hara will come to in a little while and he will be very angry with you and will

want to catch you."

At that thought Allan's blood ran cold. He could picture the big Hara in bull-like rage and the thought of himself in the grip of those hairy hands was terrifying. He stood up with Lita and looked apprehensively around.

"Which way?" he asked in a whisper.

She nodded toward the island's center. "The woods in there will be best. We'll have to avoid the village."

They started through the woods. Lita went first, her spear ready at all times. Allan followed, and after a few minutes he picked up a heavy section of hard wood that would make an effective club at need. He held the weapon awkwardly as they went on.

They were penetrating into deeper woods, and it was all a strange world to Allan. He knew forests only as seen from a flier, green masses that lay between the great cities. Now he was down in one, part of it. The birds and insects, the small animals in the brush, all of these were new to him. More than once Lita had to caution him as he made a noise in stepping on dry sticks. The girl went as quietly through the woods as a cat.

They climbed a slope and went over its ridge. On the ridge Lita halted to point out to him the clearing at the island's west end that held the village, a score or more of solid log cabins. Smoke curled from their chimneys and Allan Mann saw men standing about and children playing in the sunlit clearing. He was deeply interested by this village. But Lita led onward.

The woods about them were now so dense that Allan felt more safe. He had acquired a certain confidence of step. Then he was suddenly startled out of it. As a rabbit dashed by under their feet, bolting for cover, Lita's short spear flashed like a streak of light. The rabbit rolled over and over and then lay still.

The girl ran and picked it up, turned and held up the furry thing with her face exultant. It would be their supper, she told him. Allan stared at her incredulously. He felt as revolted by her act as his ancestors of generations before would have been by a murder. He tried not to show Lita how he regarded her.

When they reached a tiny gully deep in the woods, Lita stopped. The sun was sinking and already darkness was invading the forest. They would spend the night there, Lita told him, and she began construction of two tiny branch-shelters.

Under her orders Allan tore branches from the trees and stacked them. More than once she had to correct him and he felt ridiculously incompetent. When they had finished, before them stood two fairly tight little huts. Allan, looking at these shelters that had been brought out of nothing, for the first time felt a certain respect for the girl.

He watched her, as slowly with stone and steel she took from a pouch at her belt, she constructed a fire. He found the business of eliciting and nursing the sparks intensely engrossing. Soon she had a tiny little blaze, too small to show smoke above the darkening woods or to be seen for far.

She calmly cleaned the rabbit then. Allan watched her in entranced horror. When she had finished she began to roast it.

She offered him a red bit on a stick, to roast for himself. "I can't eat that!" he said sickly.

Lita looked at him, then smiled. "I was the same way when I came to the island," she said. "All of us are but we get to like it."

"Like eating the flesh of another living creature?" Allan said. "I'll never like that."

"You will when you're hungry enough," she said calmly, and went on roasting the rest of the rabbit.

Allan, watching her eat the browned meat, became aware that he was already very hungry. He had not eaten since that morning.

He contrasted that morning meal in the Nutrition Dispensary, with its automatic service and mushy predigested foods, with this place.

It was too dark for him to look for berries. He sat watching the girl eat. The smell of the scorched flesh, which at first he had found revolting, did not now seem so bad.

"Go ahead, eat it," Lita told him, handing him one of the roasted bits. "No matter how bad it is, it's only reasonable to eat anything that will keep you living, isn't it?"

CHAPTER III
A World of Turmoil

ALLAN'S face cleared and he nodded troubledly. It certainly was only reasonable to eat what was at hand in necessity. "I don't think I can do it, though," he said, eyeing the browned bit.

He bit gingerly into it. At the thought that he had in his mouth the flesh of another once-living creature, his stomach almost revolted. But with an effort he swallowed the bit.

It was hot and did not seem unpleasant. There were certain juices—quite unlike the foods of the Nutrition Dispensary, he thought. He reached doubtfully for another piece.

From behind her lashes with a secret smile Lita watched him eat another piece and then another of the rabbit. His jaws ached with the unaccustomed labor of chewing but his stomach sent up messages of gladness. He did not stop until all of the rabbit was gone and then he went back to some of the bones he had already discarded and polished them off more thoroughly.

He looked up at last, greasy of hands, to meet Lita's enigmatic expression. Allan flushed.

"It was only reasonable to eat all of it, since it had to be eaten," he defended.

"Did you like it?"' she said.

"What has liking got to do with the nutritive qualities of food?" he countered. Lita laughed.

They put out the fire and retired to the two huts. Lita kept her spear but he retained his club. She showed him how to close up his hut once he was inside.

For a time Allan Mann lay awake in the darkness on the branch-bed she had built. It was very uncomfortable, he found.

He could not but contrast it with his neat bed back in the dormitory that was his home in City 72. How long would it be before he was again in it, he wondered. How long—

Allan sat up, rubbing his eyes, to find bright sunlight filtering through the interstices of his leafy shelter. He had slept on the branches after all, and soundly. Yet he felt stiff and sore as he got to his feet and went out.

It was still early morning though the sunlight was bright. The other hut was empty and Lita was not anywhere in sight.

Allan felt a sudden sense of alarm. Had anything happened to his companion?

He was about to risk calling aloud when bushes rustled behind him and as he spun about she emerged from them. Her hands were full of bright red little berries.

"Breakfast," she smiled at him. "It's all there is."

They ate them. "What are we going to do now?" asked Allan.

Lita's brows knit. "I don't dare to go back to the village yet for Hara might be there. Neither can you go now after what you did."

"I don't want to go there," Allan protested quickly. He had no desire to face any more unreasonables like the one he had met.

"We'd better keep moving on into the island," she said. "We can live for a while in the woods, anyway."

They started on, the girl with her spear and Allan bringing his rude club.

The soreness and stiffness quickly left Allan's muscles as they moved on. He found a certain pleasure in this tramp through the sun-dappled woods.

They heard no sign of pursuit and relaxed their cautiousness of progress a little. It was a mistake, as Allan Mann found when something struck him a numbing blow on the left arm and he spun to find two ragged men charging fiercely from a clump of brush.

One of them had flung his club to stun Allan. The other now rushed forward with bludgeon upraised to do what his companion had failed to do. There was no possible chance to flee or to use strategy and with the blind desperate terror of a cornered animal Allan Mann struck wildly out with his own club at the on-rushing attacker.

He knocked the club spinning from the other's hand by his first wild blow. He heard Lita cry out but he was now gone amuck with terror, was showering crazy blows

upon his opponent. Then Allan became suddenly aware that the other was no longer standing before him but lay stunned at his feet. The second man was running to pick up his club.

Lita's spear flashed at the running man and missed. But as the man bent for his weapon Allan swung his club in a mighty blow.

It missed the stooping man by a foot but the terrific swing seemed to unnerve him for he abandoned his weapon and took to his heels, running back into the woods.

"Hara!" he yelled hoarsely as he ran. "Hara, here they are—!"

Lita ran to the side of the panting Allan. "You're not hurt?" she cried. "You beat them both—it was wonderful!"

But Allan Mann's sudden insanity had left him and he felt only terror. "He'll bring Hara and the rest here!" he cried. "We've got to flee—"

The girl picked up her spear and they hastened on into the forest. They heard other calling voices behind them now.

"You needn't be so afraid when you can fight like that!" Lita exclaimed as they hurried on, but Allan shook his head.

"I didn't know what I was doing! This terrible place with its fighting and turmoil and craziness—It's even got me acting as unreasonably as the others! If I ever get away from here—"

The calling voices were louder and closer behind them as the two ran on. There seemed a dozen or more of them.

Allan thought he could distinguish the bull-like voice of Hara. At thought of that red-haired giant his body went taut.

He and the girl stumbled down still another wooded slope and emerged suddenly onto an open beach, the blue sea beyond it.

"They've driven us clear to the eastern end of the island!" Allan cried. "We can't go any further and we can't hope to slip back through them!"

Lita halted, seemed to make sudden decision. "Yes, you can get back through them!" she told him. "I'll stay out here on the beach and they'll rush out toward me when they see me. It'll give you a chance to get back through the woods!"

"But I can't go like that and leave you here for Hara to capture!" said Allan in dismay.

"Why not? It wouldn't be reasonable for you to stay here and meet Hara, would it? You know what he would do to you!"

Allan shook his head troubled. "No, that wouldn't be reasonable for it wouldn't do you any good. But even though it's unreasonable I don't like to go—"

"Go and go quickly!" Lita urged, pushing him back toward the dense woods. "They'll be here in a moment!"

Allan Mann stepped reluctantly toward the woods, entered the concealing brush. He stopped, looked back to where Lita stood on the beach. He could now hear a tramp-

ing of brush as the pursuers approached.

He felt somehow that there was a defect in his reasoning, something wrong. Yet search as he might he could find nothing unreasonable in his conduct. He had never seen this girl before the preceding day, she was a life-term unreasonable, and altogether it would be completely irrational for him to imperil himself further with the atavistic Hara for her sake. This was indisputable yet—

A big form crashed through the brush close beside the hiding Allan and a triumphant bellow went up from Hara as he emerged onto the beach and saw Lita. Before she could turn on him Hara had grasped her arm, tossed her spear aside. The next instant all of Allan's faculty of reason was forgotten as with a crazy red tide of fury running through his veins he leapt out onto the beach.

"Let her go!" he yelled and charged on Hara with uplifted club.

The red-haired giant spun about, released the girl and as Allan swung in a mad blow struck out with his own club, shattering Allan's weapon with stunning force and knocking him back onto the sand.

"So it's you!" gritted Hara. He dropped his own club, clenched his huge fists. "All right, get up and take what's coming to you this time!"

Allan felt as though some resistless outside force was bringing him to his feet and hurling him toward Hara.

He saw the hard, scowling face through a red mist and then it shifted and as his clenched hand suddenly hurt him he was aware that he had struck Hara a stinging blow in the face.

Hara roared, swung furiously. Allan felt a dazing impact and then was aware that he was scrambling up again from the sand and that something warm was running over his cheek.

He flung in upon Hara and this time raised both clenched hands and hammered with them at the red-head's face.

Something hard hit his chest with stunning force, and the world, the beach, the blue sea and sky rocked wildly.

His vision cleared momentarily and he saw Hara's raging face and flailing fists, glimpsed beyond him other ragged men who were yelling as they watched, and then again the feel of hot sand on his back made him aware that he was on the ground and made him struggle up and forward.

He jabbed blindly with his fists into the red haze in which Hara's face seemed dancing. There was something running in his eyes that kept him from seeing well but it seemed to him that Hara's face was bloody.

Something colliding with his head forced him to his knees but he swayed up and struck again with both fists. Now Hara's eyes held as-tonishment as much as anger. He was backing away as Allan swung crazily.

Allan felt his strength fast running away, hunched himself and then drove forward both fists waist-high with all the weight of his body behind them. He felt smashing blows on mouth and ear as he struck, but in the next instant heard a gasp and glimpsed Hara with face gray toppling over on his side.

Then Allan was conscious of the bright sand of the beach running up to meet his face. There were men yelling and Lita's voice crying something.

He was aware of Lita's arms supporting him, her hands wiping something from his face—her hands—

Her hands became suddenly big and rough. He opened his eyes and it was not Lita at all but a white-clad guard who stood over him.

Allan stared beyond him and saw not beach and sea but the metal-walled interior of a small flier. He could see the back of a pilot sitting in the nose of the craft and could hear the roar of air outside.

"Conscious at last, eh?" said the guard. "You've been out for half an hour."

"But where—how—" Allan struggled to say.

"You don't remember?" the guard said. "I'm not surprised—you were just passing out when we got there. You see, your sentence on the island was only one day. We came to get you and found you'd apparently been having trouble with one of the other unreasonables, but we picked you up and started back. We're almost back to City 72 now."

Allan Mann sat up, utterly dismayed. "But Lita!. Where's Lita?"

The guard stared. "You mean the girl unreasonable who was there? Why, she's still there, of course. She's a lifer. She made quite a fuss when we dropped down and got you."

"But I don't want to leave Lita there!" cried Allan. "I tell you, I don't want to leave her!"

"Don't want to leave her?" repeated the astonished guard. "Listen, you're being unreasonable again. If you keep it up you'll get another sentence to the island and it'll be more than a day!"

Allan looked keenly at him. "You mean that if I'm unreasonable enough they'd send me back to the island—for life?"

"They sure would!" the guard declared. "You're mighty lucky to get off with one day there this time."

Allan Mann did not answer nor did he speak again until their destination was reached and he faced the Director once more.

The Director looked at his bruised face and smiled. "Well, it seems that even one day on the island has taught you what it is to live without reason," he said.

"Yes, it's taught me that," Allan answered.

"I am glad of that," the Director told him. "You realize now that my only motive in sending you there was to cure you of unreasonable tendencies."

Allan nodded quietly. "It would be about the most unreasonable thing possible for me to resent your efforts to cure and help me, wouldn't it?"

The Director smiled complacently. "Yes, my boy, that would certainly be the height of unreason."

"I thought it would," said Allan Mann in the same quiet voice.

His fist came back

The guards were wholly unsympathetic as their flier sped with Allan Mann for a second time toward the island.

"It's your own fault you got a life-sentence on the island," the chief guard said. "Whoever heard of anyone doing such a crazy thing as knocking down a Director?"

But Allan, unlistening, was gazing eagerly ahead. "There it is!" he bawled joyfully. "There's the island!"

"And you're glad to get back?" The chief guard gave up in disgust. "Of all the unreasonables we ever carried, you're the worst."

The flier sank down through the warm afternoon sunlight and poised again above the sandy beach.

Allan leapt out and started up the beach. He did not hear what the guard shouted as the flier rose and departed.

Nor did he look after it as it vanished this time. He pressed along the beach and then through the woods toward the island's western end.

He came into the clearing where was the village of cabins. There were people in the clearing and one of them saw Allan Mann, ran toward him with a glad cry. It was a girl—it was Lita!

They met and somehow Allan found it natural to be holding her in the curve of his arm as she clung to him.

"They took you away this morning!" she was crying. "I thought you'd never come back—"

"I've come back to stay," Allan told her. "I'm a lifer now, too." He said it almost proudly.

"You a lifer?" Rapidly he told her what he had done. "I didn't want to stay back there. I like it better here!" he finished.

"So you're back, are you?" It was Hara's bull-voice that sounded close beside them and Allan spun with a snarl on his lips.

But Hara was grinning across all his battered face as he came forward and extended his hand to Allan. "I'm glad that you're back! You're the first man ever to knock me out and I like you!"

Allan stared dazedly. "But you surely don't like me because I did that? It's not reasonable—"

A chorus of laughs from the men and women gathered around cut him short. "Remember that you're living on the island of unreason, lad!" cried Hara.

"But Lita?" exclaimed Allan.

"You can't have her—you—"

"Calm yourself," advised Hara with a grin. He beckoned and a pert blond girl came out of the others to him. "Look what was left by a flier while you were gone, and with a life-sentence too. I forgot all about Lita when I saw her, didn't I, darling?"

"You'd better," she advised him, and then smiled at Allan. "We're getting married this evening."

"Married?" he repeated, and Hara nodded.

"Sure, by the old ceremonies like we use here. We've a religious preacher here that was sent here because religion's unreasonable too, and he performs them."

Allan Mann turned to the girl in his arm, a great new idea dawning across his brain. "Then Lita, you and I—"

That evening after the double marriage had been performed and those in the village were engaged in noisy and completely irrational merrymaking, Allan and Lita sat with Hara and his bride on a bluff at the island's western end, looking toward the last glow of sunset's red embers in the darkening sky.

"Some day," said Hara, "when there's a lot more of us unreasonables we'll go back there and take the world and make it all unreasonable and inefficient and human again."

"Some day—" Allan murmured.

THE END

NEWSCAST

By Harl Vincent

Inventor Tom Burke built a polyceltron iconoscope—and synchronized sound and vision to scandal-blast a city-wide political intrigue with his all-permeating broadcast televisor!

SLOUCHED in his overstuffed chair behind the desk, Emmett Graves sat tapping the polished mahogany surface before him with pudgy fingers while he stared at the blank rectangle of the newscast receiver on the opposite wall. There had been an interruption in the service for two minutes and he looked often and angrily at his ornate platinum watch. In eight more minutes the sports flash was due to go on. Meanwhile, this war news—most important of all—was ruined. Unless it came on again at once.

"Young fool ought to be back on police court work!" Graves raged impotently. He rolled the frayed end of a black cigar from one side of his thick-lipped mouth to the other.

Miss Hennessey, his pretty secretary, tiptoed into the room, laid a sheaf of papers before him and noiselessly disappeared. Just as well, Graves reflected grumpily. She was too high-hat, Miss Hennessey was—she'd refused him dinner dates, theatres, even had given his flowers to one of the stenographers in the outer office. He'd have to fire her and get a new one.

But this service interruption was more important at the moment than any secretary, whether she high-hatted him or not. As President of International Newscasts, the pompous little fat man was taking his job very much to heart for the first time in many moons. Tommy Burke, his star reporter, had fallen down on him. And usually Burke was not one to do a thing like this unless the reason was a mighty important one. Well, he'd fire him too if this interruption continued for long.

Three minutes, four—five! A check showed him that All-World Newscasts still had the war flash on. With a wrathful grunt, Graves put a blunt fingertip on Miss Hennessey's call button. The girl was at his side so quickly and soundlessly that he started visibly.

"Get Burke on the radiophone," he directed, mopping his double chin with a lavendar silk handkerchief, "and get him quick. Ask the blasted idiot what's wrong with the newscast."

"Tommy is at the front," Miss Hennessey reminded him.

"Oh, Tommy it is? So that's the way the wind blows." Graves glared at the girl, then shook himself deeper into his chair. "Well, get our Tampico station then and have

Burke could barely see through his view finder to train his lens upon the troops

them get through to him via the Loyalist Signal Corps. You can do it in a minute if you don't stand there dreaming. Hurry now."

"Yes, Mr. Graves." Again the silent departure.

But the battle front was never reached by radiophone, nor did that one particular newscast resume. The portly President of International nearly died of apoplexy in the next long moments. All-World had made a complete scoop for ten important minutes.

Entirely out of God's knowledge, in the hottest battle sector in central Mexico, Burke had been televising and picking up the sound, not to speak sending in the frequent announcements of what was to be learned of the fighting in other sectors. This was nothing new to Burke; he was a veteran at war reporting and was as much excited by it all as if he had been a combatant. And he had never quite gotten over the thrill of knowing that, all over the world, millions were seeing the results of his camera work and hearing the yells and rumblings of guns, the shrieking and detonations of shells which were picked up by his banks of microphones. And loving it too, these millions. Bloodthirsty to the last one of them. Especially when sitting snugly and safely at home before their own private newscast receivers or when lounging in one of the public squares where International had installed huge mirror screens and amplifiers and where the roar of battle could be heard as loudly as at the front.

NO, Burke did not mind. Not that way. But he had been here too long now; the monotony was beginning to tell on him. Besides he was most anxious to get back to New York— there was that invention of his to perfect and it was an important one. Burke was a real scientific experimenter, only keeping to his reporting so he could pay the freight.

"That puffy old lady-killer," he told his radio man, "ought to be out *here* for a while. I'd love to see him in a gas mask, to see him turn tail and waddle away from the creeper clouds."

"Who? What?" The radio man removed his headphones.

Burke had come back to the twin short wave transmitter from his own televising camera and micro-phone banks. The transmitter was a good two hundred feet behind the front line trenches for a measure of greater safety. Much good that did at times!

"Graves. The stubborn ox. Doesn't even answer my radiograms."

The radio man grinned crookedly. He knew how anxious the tall young reporter was to return to the States. "Better get back up in front," he said. Then he watched the lanky figure as it stooped and crept through the communicating trench, tin hat askew, gas mask and holster dangling from his belt, boots caked with mud. Burke was a good scout.

Dropping into his cubby off the front trench, the reporter checked the focus of his telephoto lens through the periscope at the top of which it was mounted. The image it projected on the plate of the pickup tube was perfect.

He swung the periscope around, sweeping the Rebels' front lines and the narrow strip of pockmarked land which lay between the two lines. If this was what the newscast public wanted, let them have it. Suddenly he was alert; his view finder showed a thick red cloud rolling eerily up from nowhere and spreading. A creeper cloud! The signal for gas masks came down the trench. Burke had his on in a jiffy.

Captain Volez swept past him, running.

"What's doing?" the reporter

called to him in Spanish.

"A charge—coming. Good picture."

The sound of the heavy artillery, the shrieking and bursting of HE shells, the rat-tat of machine guns rose to a deafening roar. The sound of the planes overhead was an unbelievable clamor. Mud flung high as a barrage was laid down by the Rebels ahead of the creeper cloud. These deadly gases could be dispersed by flame projectors if their fusible elements could be reached by the licking, searing blasts. "Modern warfare" was pretty much the same old stuff, Burke reflected. Just bigger guns, more powerful explosives, deadlier gases.

Loyalist troops streamed through the trench behind him, bound for the point where the sally was headed. The creeper cloud came on. The barrage was in the trenches, then had passed beyond. A clang and a heavy blow on the reporter's helmet drove him to his knees and nearly deafened him. He had a charmed life.

The red gas rolled down now upon the Loyalists, filled the trench. Burke could barely see through his view finder to train his lens upon the charging Rebel troops. Oh, the newscast hounds would eat this up!

CRASH! The view finder was driven painfully against his cheek. He looked up at the top of his periscope and saw it was gone. So was a perfectly good F-0. 9 telephoto lens, the

third one in a week at six hundred smacks a copy. Burke swore softly as he went back through the communicating trench.

The indescribable ear-splitting whistle of an HE shrilled overhead, too close for comfort. Burke flattened himself instinctively. Then, Whang! All Hell seemed to break loose. Mud, rocks, debris, rained on the prostrate reporter. That one *was* close. Painfully he dragged himself from the mess encumbering him, slowly he crawled back toward the transmitter.

Where it had been a deep crater, still smoking. Twisted bits of wire, fragments of glass, were all that remained of the twin radio apparatus. A dismembered crumpled form thrown up on the edge of the crater told him what had become of that decent little radio engineer. Burke swore feelingly.

"Damn Graves anyway!" He made his way over the top, ducked into another communicating trench and started for the rear. "I've told the fathead a dozen times to install the transmitters in fast armored tanks. God knows *they* cost enough to replace. But you can't replace the poor guys that run them. I'm going home—to hell with Graves."

A Loyalist army plane whisked him to Mexico City in two hours. From here Burke sent a radiogram to Graves:

"Am taking next stratoplane home. Lenses and transmitters don't grow on trees. Neither do swell radio engineers. And there are no trees where we were. Hope, it hurts you a lot to accept this collect. I'll make it long and expensive. Will be home in a few hours but am going to get a good night's sleep and will see you in the morning in good little, dear little old New York. My best regards to Miss Hennessey. Has she accepted your customary dinner invitation yet? I hope not, for her sake. Burke."

If Graves had been purple with near-apoplexy before, he was almost black when this radio reached his desk a few hours after the trouble with the war newscast. He reached for his vacuum bottle, found it empty of ice water.

"Miss Hennessey!" he shouted, forgetting even to ring for her. "What's the matter with the thermos bottle. Get me some ice water."

"Yes, Mr. Graves." The girl had whisked away the bottle and was returning with it refilled before he had mopped the perspiration from his creased brow.

"You're fired!" he roared at her.

"Oh, thank you, Mr. Graves,"—sweetly. "That means two weeks' pay is coming to me. Thank you again. I already have a new position with All-World. Will you sign this voucher, please?"

Miss Hennessey, not now so sweet and pretty in Graves's glazed eye, thrust a paper before him. It was an order for two weeks' pay ahead, on account of her release by him. The little vixen had already filled it out.

"But—but—"

"Sign right here, Mr. Graves." His erstwhile secretary did not use such dulcet tones this time.

Graves signed, noting the glint in the girl's yellow eyes, then sank back in his chair exhausted. These youngsters would be the death of him yet. All-World. Damned upstart outfit; they'd not get the best of Emmett Graves nor of International.

He turned in disgust from the "Every Day a New Menu" newscast and flipped the switch which shut off the uninteresting sight of a scrawny woman mixing a most appetizing—but not to him—salad, and the sound of her shrill, monotonous voice as well. He'd have to do some more firing. This feature could go to All-World for all he cared.

Again he looked at Burke's radiogram, snorted, crumpled it in a tight ball and deposited it carefully in his wastebasket. Then he looked once more at his expensive timepiece. After five it was! Holy Smoke! Mrs. Graves would jump down his throat. He became a volcano of activity, crammed his hat on his head, turned out the lights and scurried for the elevator.

BURKE arrived at his combined laboratory and bachelor quarters late that night. After a luxurious bath and shave, he went at once to the laboratory and dusted off his beloved apparatuses. For the time, Graves, the Mexican Revolution—everything—was forgotten. He had something here which would revolutionize newscasting—maybe. At any rate it was something worth working on and bringing to the point of perfection. He worked all night with his special televising camera, his pick-ups and the recording apparatus. And with something that looked suspiciously like an x-ray.

None the worse for his months of grueling war experience and the loss of another night of sleep, he appeared bright and early in the morning at the mid-town headquarters of International. He breezed into Graves's outer office with his usually unruly mop of blond hair slicked meticulously back and with a gaudy cravat conspicuous under his opened lapels. Burke never wore a hat nor did he care much about his personal appearance. He whistled as he entered.

The whistle dwindled from a defiant one to a very subdued sound, a mere chirp of sheer amazement. For a girl sat on one of the benches where Graves usually kept them waiting; a real dream, she was. Blue eyes, hollowed underneath—peaches and cream complexion—a pert, upturned nose—saucy red lips. But she was painfully thin, her dress was shabby, and her funny little hat a mess from the rain of the night before. Obviously this girl was on her uppers, just what old Graves was always looking for.

Taking an even closer look, Burke made up his mind then and there that this was one girl the old man would not make a fool of. He stalked to her side and asked

boldly: "Anything I can do for you, Miss?"

"Why, do you work here?"—coolly.

"I haven't any hat on, have I?" Burke's smile was infectious and the girl didn't know that he always went hatless.

She smiled wanly. "Well," she faltered, "I'm looking for a job. It was on the public newscast last night—'Secretary Wanted,'—so I came to see about it."

"I'm just the man you want to see," the reporter told her. "If you'll wait a few minutes in this conference room I'll be with you."

Unhesitatingly she followed him. Burke closed her in the small room and went to bang on the boss's door. No secretary was in the outer office.

"Come in!" blared the little big man's voice. Burke went in.

"Morning, Graves," blithely. "Where's Hennessey?"

"Fired. Same as you'll be. What do you mean 'Morning?', you jackanapes? What'd that crazy radio of yours mean? Twenty-eight dollars it cost International." Graves banged on his desk.

THE reporter grinned. "Keep your shirt on, boss. You can do your blowing off after I've finished. I'm through in Mexico. No more for me. Know your last transmitter down there was blown to Kingdom Come yesterday and a dam' good radio man with it? I'll not take another of these assignments until you see the tanks for them like I told you. Three lenses in a week—of course that's not so bad. Eighteen hundred smackers doesn't mean as much to you as twenty-eight for a radiogram you damn well deserved. Not for lenses—as long as your newscasts are on the air. I'm through I tell you."

Again the banging of the desk top. "You're telling me!" Graves bleated. "You're fired. Draw your pay and get out."

"Oke. But you didn't tell me about Hennessey. Fire her, too?"

"Yes, if it's any of your business."

"Couldn't make her, eh?" Burke's voice held deep loathing.

"Get out, I say Get out!" Apoplexy threatened once more.

The reporter retired to the little conference room, where he took the blue-eyed girl by the arm. "Come on," he said, "we have to go to another office. We'll talk over the job there." He found she needed some assistance in getting to her feet. Why, the poor kid was starved!

She followed him without question and Burke was glad that Graves had not started out from his private office after him. Other girls were now in line in the anteroom for the actual position.

"What's your name?" he asked the girl in the elevator.

"Nina Cowan."

"Nina." Burke sort of rolled the name over his tongue.

"And my experience," she began, "has been—"

"We'll let that go until later. Had any breakfast?"

"Why—why—"

"You haven't. Neither have I. We'll eat first."

"But." They were on the street now and Burke was piloting her into one of his favorite haunts.

"No buts. We eat."

THEY ate, the girl ravenously, Burke observed. Color was starting to return to her cheeks and her eyes looked brighter already.

"You haven't told me who you are?" she reminded him as they sat over their coffee.

Burke told her.

"Oh, I've listened to your newscasts often. They're the best—"

"Forget it," the reporter interrupted. "It's up to me to confess. I was just fired from International and I want to put you to work—for me."

Nina Cowan stood up suddenly, "But it was Graves who wanted a secretary. You've deceived me."

"Listen now; Graves is a bum. All he thinks of is running around with his secretaries. That's why the last one was fired. You're too darned nice for—"

"I can handle that sort. But not a liar. Good-bye, *Mister* Burke. I'm going back and get that job. Thanks for the eats."

Nina Cowan was gone and with her going the sun seemed to set and the day become gloomy. Burke paid his check and left for his uptown quarters.

Work is a cure-all sometimes. Burke worked as he had never done before for the next few days. But he did not forget Nina Cowan. He checked up with some of his old pals at International and learned that she had landed the job with the Old Man. He hated to think of her in that office, of the Old Man's pawings. With Hennessey, now, it had been different—that had merely struck him funny. Hennessey was a nice enough kid, of course. But Nina was somehow different. He could have wrung her neck cheerfully at this point.

He immersed himself more deeply in his work. The laboratory was a shamble of coils, condensers, vacuum tubes, batteries, and built-over motor-generator sets. A standard newscast receiver stood unused against one wall. Burke was working on the pickup end of the apparatus.

Late in the afternoon of the fifth day after his dismissal by Graves, he suddenly jumped up from his work and sent a long and carefully written radiogram to the chief of the Federal Bureau of Investigation in Washington. He had something at last, he knew. One last little touch and it was to be perfect. The standard newscast pickup apparatus was entirely satisfactory, of course, but it was bulky. The camera itself was a simple affair, using a huge polyceltron vacuum tube with an eight by ten plate on which the images from its fast lens were projected. The dark and light images produced the myriads of impulses required for transmission by radio on one frequency while the sound impulses from the microphones were transmitted on a second frequency. The result in simultaneously tuned reception and reproduction was as perfect as could be desired. But the experimenter was after important improvements.

Burke had always wanted something compact. More than that he was obsessed with the idea of producing perfect recordings of sound and vision pickups simultaneously so they could be reproduced at any time desired. This had not yet been done successfully, due to various factors that made synchronization difficult. Then there was a problem of televising and sound pickup in places difficult of access. That was where the modified x-ray came in. The only thing now holding him back was an ultra-sensitive microphone that would not blast.

He had just about reached the solution when his buzzer roused him from his work. This was five days after his dismissal by Graves.

Burke sauntered to his door in carpet slippers and shirt sleeves, with three days' growth of beard ornamenting his jowls. It was Nina!

The girl pushed past him into the room. She was flushed and excited. "You were right—Tommy. And I was wrong. I'm sorry."

The reporter's jaw set. "Graves try anything funny?"

"Y—yes. And I quit. Your job still open for me?"

"Oughtn't to be, young lady,"—sternly. "You took a run-out powder on me, you know."

"Oh, I *am* sorry. When can I go to work?"

Burke had to grin in spite of himself. "Now. Sixty a week. I have a. flock of notes I want typed up. Here, this way. And don't think I'll try to get fresh, either."

He led her to the typewriter desk in the laboratory, handed her a jumbled mass of scribbled sheets and told her to go ahead. Then, a wave of embarrassment sweeping over him, he returned feverishly to his own work. The click of the typewriter was music to his ears.

From time to time the girl watched him from the corner of her eye. He did not know she was noting his every move with avid interest. But she caught him several times when he stole glances at her.

And when finally, with headphones clamped tightly to his ears, he yelped, "I've got it!" she came flying to the workbench.

"Got what?" she demanded.

"*It*. The last link in the chain. Now we *have* something."

Nina Cowan sat on a high stool at his side, staring at the—to her—bewildering array of mechanisms. "Tell me all about it," she pleaded.

BURKE had kept his ideas pent up for so long that it was great to confide in someone. And no confidant could have been more welcome than Nina Cowan. "Sure," he enthused. "I'll expound."

He expounded. Four mechanisms there were, each like nothing the girl had ever seen. Burke enclosed them separately in leather cases with carrying straps. He picked up the smallest of the four, which was only a handful to carry, pointed it at the girl's curly head. She saw it had a big twinkling eye of a lens.

"This," he told her, "is my camera."

"A televisor?"

"Nothing else. And the side—this bump you see—is the regular microphone which picks up ordinary sound."

"Now, wait a minute," the girl broke in. "Tell me how the modern television operates. I've always wanted to know. Maybe I'm a dumb-Dora but I've seen the cameras and microphones and of course plenty of different sorts of receivers. Still I don't get it."

"Perfectly simple." And it was not simple at all to Nina, though Burke clumsily tried to make it so. "Here's a lens that projects an image. What on?—a plate in a vacuum tube. Iconoscopes, they used to call these tubes before they were perfected for color. The plate in this tube catches the image, converts it into electrical impulses and—"

"Wait a minute. How?"

"Aw, easy. The plate is divided into five hundred lines of tiny cells over which the light beam travels sixty times a second from bottom to top, because the lens inverts the image."

"Skip it," Nina said wearily. "I'll

never get it in a million years."

"Okay—I thought you wanted to know." Burke picked up his miniature televisor.

"Mean to tell me this little thing takes the place of the huge cameras the reporters use? The ones that take two men to carry them and have a truck following them?"

"Sure. My polyceltron tube has the same number of cells in a one by one and a half inch plate as the big ones do in eight by ten. And here is my truck."

Burke strapped a larger case to his belt and attached it to the wires of the televisor and built-in mike. "This is no transmitter," he explained, "but a voice and vision recorder which magnetically and permanently writes down on a metallic tape the electrical impulses from the tiny polyceltron in the camera and from the voice amplifiers. At any time or from any standard transmitter these impulses can be sent out as perfectly synchronized newscasts. Or, for that matter, this recorder can be used for the theatrical telecasts if this should prove to be desirable."

"All right, Mr. Professor; can present happenings be kept in a little roll of metal tape and reproduced a hundred years from now?"

"A thousand years, if necessary." Burke was showing the workings of his apparatus.

"Hm. Good stuff," the girl commented. "But not for newscasts."

"Right." Burke grinned at her perspicacity. "The news hound wants the news when it happens, not in a thousand years."

"Then what's the object?"

Again the experimenter grinned. Nina was a smart girl. "There is a still more important field. You haven't seen the half."

He removed the third mechanism from its case and set it close to the wall, wiring it to the first two. There was a whir and he raised the camera to eye level, aiming its lens at the blank wall.

"You don't by any chance think you're taking a picture?" the girl asked him.

"Sure. Now watch." The fourth case was opened and more wires appeared. A small cable led to a round case with a rubber suction cup which Burke moistened and attached to the steel wall. Once more the whirring started. "And sound as well, unheard sound," he added.

In a few minutes he shut off the power and removed a small reel from the case at his belt. "This," he told her, "is a complete record of what has been going on in the next room."

"You see," he intoned, "the vision goes out on an extremely high frequency, the sound on a much lower one. In ordinary news or telecast reception no difference is noted by eye or ear in the lag between the two widely different waves. But in a recording that lag has always until now presented difficulties. Now we—"

"Shoot it," the girl directed. Her eyes brightened with more than comprehension, bluer than ever.

BURKE inserted the reel in what looked to be a short wave radio transmitter. Then he dimmed the lights of the room and turned on his newscast receiver. "It only takes impulses from my own transmitter now," he explained.

In a moment the vision screen lighted. Flickerless and clear, there was the view of the next room. A modern living room, where a man sat at a table eating his dinner. It was perfect—and taken through a steel wall. The man laid down his knife as a woman came in and sat across from him. Still there was no sound, though the lips of both were moving in speech. Nina recalled that Burke had not turned on the sound recorder in the beginning. That was what the case with the suction cup was for—it picked up the sound beyond the wall. It must have tremendous sensitivity. Without its help nothing could be heard through that sound-proof partition with its deadening layer between the two vertical sheets of metal.

Then it was there, the speech of the man and the woman, the clatter of knives and forks and dishes. Petty table conversation, that of almost any average man and wife at dinner. But clear and lifelike as if transmitted from one of the huge stations of International or All-World. And with this diminutive and revolutionary equipment which could see all and hear all.

The girl gasped as Burke switched off his apparatus and the lights of the laboratory came on. "I see now what you're driving at," she exclaimed delightedly. "You've got something here."

Burke wondered amazedly whether she *did* see.

"I think so,"—soberly. Then he handed her a radiogram that he had just received from Washington. "And now, Ni—Miss Cowan—please read this and answer it at once—just a short formal acceptance."

When he saw her look of amazement as she sat before her typewriter reading the radiogram, he knew she did understand.

"After that we'll see Graves," Burke concluded. "You and I alone together. We'll see him about lots of things."

The pair sauntered nonchalantly into Graves' outer office, Nina gamely insisting on carrying the case which housed the penetrating ray generator. Burke, with the other cases, winked at Gloria Fay, the redheaded reception clerk.

"Who's with the Old Man?" he asked her.

"Only the Mayor and his Better Housing Committee. Why—and why the Christmas tree effect?"

"Oh, these are bombs," Burke assured her, patting his three cases. "Mind if we go in and blow up the Old Man?"

"See if I care. Bust right in." The Fay woman chewed her gum violently, then added, "There's a bunch of dames after the secretary job again—waiting." She looked significantly at Nina.

"Perfect," said the erstwhile reporter. "Come on, Nina."

They passed the line of waiting applicant, some pretty, some not so hot. All of them looked anxious. Graves would have a lot of fun with this assortment—if he could. He always tried hard enough.

BURKE strode to the outer wall of the Old Man's office with Nina at his heels. The line of waiting women observed them curiously, probably setting them down as a repair crew. Burke set up the four mechanisms, attached his supersensitive microphone to the wall, and switched on the juice. He kept his tiny camera moving in a slow arc to cover the interior of the room behind that double insulated steel wall—to cover all of it. The recorder whirred on.

Soon there were stirrings within, voices that now could be heard through the uninsulated door as men came to its inner knob. Rattling of the latch. Burke switched off his power supply.

"Come on," he told Nina. "Let's move."

They moved, lounging over to a window of the outer office that overlooked the river.

Filing from. Graves' office were some of the most prominent dignitaries of the city, most of them looking rather sheepish. One of the waiting girl applicants for the secretarial position, probably the most attractive of the lot, was called into the sanctum sanctorum.

Burke rushed to his instruments as soon as the door closed behind her. The Fay woman had approached and was looking interestedly over his shoulder. "Go away," he said. "This is going to be good. But not yet—there's nothing to see for a while."

The penetrating ray and the weaving camera lens—a gleaming bull's eye of optical glass almost as large as the televisor itself—were in action only a few minutes when out rushed the girl who had entered the room. She was red of face and disheveled of hair.

"Swell!" exulted Burke. "Come on, Nina." He grabbed up his instruments hastily.

Another of the applicants had been called for, but Burke winked at Gloria again suggestively and strode into the Old Man's office instead, with Nina trotting contentedly at his side.

Graves looked at the two in purpled astonishment. His fat fist began to hammer on the desk as his former reporter bolted the door from inside. "What in the devil?" he spouted. "The two of you—so help me—together! You've a nerve."

"Keep your shirt on," Burke counseled. "We've something to show you. Something worth while to you. Something worth while to International, interesting to the entire world. My own invention."

"Oh, all right." Graves had never been one to pass up a chance of a patent steal. There had been many of these, as Burke well knew but could not have proved. "What is it? But make it snappy."

The political newscasts were on the large receiver. Burke turned them off. "Now," he said, "cut out your regular frequencies and plug me in on the local shorts. Got to show you this."

Surprisingly, Graves complied.

The whir of Burke's recorder lighted up the screen and started the sound. The President of International Newscasts gasped when he saw himself pictured right here at his own desk and heard the words of raw political intrigue he had exchanged with the Mayor and his Committee. If this ever went out over the air it would mean utter ruin. . . .

" Shut it off. Name your price."

"There isn't any price." Burke shifted the tape.

HERE was the Old Man desperately trying to make love to the last applicant for what he called a position. His foolish words of pseudo-endearment made Nina giggle.

"Shut it off!" Graves's pleading was panicky. "If Mrs. Graves ever should see *this* recording."

Burke was grinning down at him. "Enough?" he asked. "Going to be good now?"

"It's enough." Graves nodded, then looked up, white-faced. "Ten thousand dollars for your invention," he offered. "Why, International can expose all sorts of things with this. Your jobs back, too, both

of you—at twice your last salary. Is it a bargain?"

Nina sniffed. "A bargain! It isn't even interesting."

Burke was slinging his cases over his shoulder and to his belt. "No go." he said. "International expose things? You're crazy. Just newshound stuff is what you want. Blood and thunder stuff to keep the sheep in line, to make International the superior of All-World. You don't know from nothing, Graves. Let this just be a lesson to you—no price connected with it. Except you've got to put those front line transmitters in tanks like I told you."

"I will, I will. Anything! But—but —you won't turn this invention of yours over to All-World."

"A better place than that. To the Federal Bureau of Investigation in Washington."

"Not this reel you just showed?" Graves surely would die of his bursting veins.

Nina and Burke were at the door and Graves waddled after them most ludicrously. "*Please*, Burke— you know me—you had a good job with me. I'll do anything. If my wife—"

"Yes, I know you." Burke laughed. "Don't worry. I'll not turn in this reel yet—I'll just keep it to make sure you behave yourself from now on. You're on probation— with me, now. It's about time the newscasters of this country kept out of crooked politics."

Waiting for the elevator at the

reception desk, Nina hugged close to Burke's side. "Won't it be grand?" she said. "In Washington, with your new G-man job, we can live *swell*. You'll be in something you can be proud of—and *I'll* have a man to be proud of."

Burke reddened—stammered.

"M—mean it?" Nina was proposing to him! He'd have never had the nerve himself.

"Course I mean it—Silly." Her bright eyes looked up into his astonished ones invitingly.

And the Fay woman almost swallowed her gum when she saw Tommy Burke lift the little blue-eyed girl from her feet and kiss her resoundingly on lips that obviously were most receptive.

THE END

INVISIBLE

By Eric Frank Russell

Mason thought invisibility made him the perfect criminal!

HASTILY putting down the green vial "Shorty" Mason flopped upon the settee. His legs twitched, his fingers trembled uncontrollably. The serum from the vial was a veritable hell's brew. He could feel it searing inside, shooting like heated mercury through his tortured veins.

"Highly radioactive," Professor Dainton had said.

It had meant nothing to Mason then but it meant a lot now.

Shorty lay back, sweat beading his forehead, while Pepito, the professor's Mexican hairless dog, made weird noises out in the yard. According to Dainton's estimate the liquid from the vial should take effect in half an hour. It had taken only fifteen minutes to perform its work on the dog.

Agony gave way to a dull listless ache accompanied by sensations of effervescence in the bloodstream. Mason looked at his naked legs, saw no alteration in their appearance. He stretched his nude form full length and pondered while he waited. Shorty Mason was on his uppers but with the means to easy money right at hand—Dainton unwittingly had provided the means.

If Dainton had not got himself run over by a car there would have been no need for Mason to take a chance with the scientist's discovery. But Dainton was dead and it was up to Mason to give the stuff in the vial its first chance to work on a human being. What it did to Pepito it could do to him, he felt certain.

Only the previous Wednesday he and the professor had stood in the backyard and observed Pepito after he had been inoculated with the serum. The dog had scuttled around with its customary joyful genuflexions but neither of them could follow its movements. For the dog had become invisible.

Stealing another look at his legs Mason found them becoming diaphanous, indefinite. He blinked, looked again, smiled grimly as he realized the experiment was going to succeed.

TEN minutes later he stood in front of a full-length mirror, stroking a closely shaved head that could not be seen, feeling smooth legs that were not apparent in the glass. Perfect mimicry!

What the chameleon could do in a couple of hours his body could do instantaneously and with complete faithfulness.

He heard the bullet moan
across his shoulder

His chest reproduced the batik pattern of the wallpaper behind him. His feet and ankles simulated the grained oak skirting board. When he moved the patterns moved in reverse and held their relative positions. The whole thing was incredible, yet true—the truth evident in the empty mirror. He had made himself transparent—invisible to the normal eye.

He had thought Dainton foolish enough when the latter picked him up at the prison gates and gave him a new start as an assistant. He had been certain that Dainton was unbalanced when he found that the scientist's sole object in life was to satisfy his curiosity about chameleons. Looking at the blank mirror he knew that Dainton had been quite mad to devote half a lifetime to the development of something that was of no practical use except to crooks.

The old investigator had talked a lot about his eccentric work. Once he had handed Mason a photograph of a blossom-laden bush.

"Some of those are flowers, others are not," he had said. "They look like blossoms but they aren't."

"What are they then?" Shorty had asked.

"Examples of perfect mimicry," the professor had replied. "They are clusters of plant-sucking Phormnia, insects of the Fulgoridae family. Individually, they look like tiny plume-backed wax-coated porcupines of the insect world and they are found in the Bengal Dooars and the jungles of Assam. Their mimicry is so truthful that even birds, perching on the same branch, can be deceived."

Mason had gaped at the photograph, tried hard to discern which blooms were really blooms and which were insects. It was impossible to tell.

"Countless centuries of evolution moulded that protective ability," the professor had declared, "yet the chameleon can exercise similar powers in a mere couple of hours and adapt the effect to circumstances."

"So what?" had been Mason's query.

"It is a longer jump from a million years to a couple of hours than it is from a couple of hours to a split second." A determined gleam in his eyes, Dainton had added, "What I am seeking is the secret of instantaneous camouflage!"

Then Dainton had plunged into a long involved speech about chameleons employing some glandular substance that could do to the atoms and molecules of the epidermis what adrenalin could do to the heart. He had talked about chameleons speeding up their vibratory rate until they were reflecting those frequencies of the spectrum compatible with their surroundings. He

thought the process could be improved, perfected. Mason had dutifully agreed without having the faintest idea of what all the talk was about.

But now he knew that Dainton had found success on the eve of his death. How the formula functioned Mason neither knew nor cared. The effect was what he wanted.

Bending toward the mirror Mason saw the faint outline of himself. It was difficult to discern. He decided that he could see it because he was standing still and his surface was nearer to the glass than was the surface he was imitating.

Taking a hand-mirror he turned around and surveyed his back. It reproduced the batik. All sides of him merged into their respective backgrounds, regardless of the angles from which they were viewed. To all intents and purposes he was an invisible man.

Satisfied, Mason decided that now was the time to collect the John Legattrick Company's payroll and thus turn another scientific achievement to the practical use of crime.

At the front door force of habit drove his hand toward his hat and coat. He resisted the impulse and paused with his fingers on the door-lock. The hall mirror gave him the confidence he required to step into the street stark naked. He set his heavy jaw, opened the door and boldly stepped out.

The street was drab and sullen beneath the hidden sun but the air was warm enough to compensate for Mason's lack of clothes. A fat little man hurried along the sidewalk, his feet pattering on the shadowless concrete.

He headed straight toward Mason, his eyes studying the dull horizon, his mind occupied to the exclusion of all else. Mason dodged him with a thrill of apprehension, rapidly followed by a feeling of intense relief. The fat man trotted on.

FOURTH Avenue was like a game of tag with a million blindfolded players. Mason had to sneak around standing people, sidestep walkers and jump from the paths of men in a hurry. Several times he narrowly avoided a betraying bump. Once he barely escaped being run over by a taxi.

The clock over the First Federal Bank said two minutes to eleven when Mason reached its doors. He had timed himself beautifully. Within two or three minutes a cashier and an armed guard would arrive to claim the Legattrick weekly payroll of forty thousand dollars.

A glance at the still-clouded sky—then Mason jumped for a compartment in the bank's revolving door, entering close behind an unsuspecting customer. Moving to the farther wall he walked to and fro while he waited. His body was marble against the marble slabs. His constant motion permitted no peculiarity in perspective that might arouse suspicion in the sharp-eyed.

Forty thousand dollars was a nice little sum, he mused. A smart fellow could get around with a wad that size. All he had to do was take it, run like blazes and hide it in a safe spot from which it could be retrieved later. He had marked out such a place a mere three hundred yards away.

Once he'd dumped the money his pursuers—if any—would have nothing visible to pursue. It was the easiest stunt in the whole history of larceny—and the green vial held enough doses for a dozen more similar exploits. Mason ceased his pondering as the bank's door spun at the stroke of eleven.

A man came through the door, a lumpy man with a big leather bag grasped in his right fist. He was followed by a lean lanky fellow whose sharp eyes flickered beneath the visor of his peaked cap and who carried a shoulder holster prominently in view. The first was the John Legattrick Company's cashier—the other his bodyguard.

Both men walked across the floor to the glass holes yawning above the counter. The first man dumped his bag on the mahogany and pushed a paper through a gap in the bulletproof glass. The bodyguard hung around and chewed his fingernails.

Rolls of coinage were shoved across the counter, checked on a slip held by the lumpy man, then placed in his bag. Finally came the paper money in the form of a flat square packet. Legattrick's cashier reached for it—and grasped air.

The bundle clutched in his sweating right hand, Mason raced madly for the door. None could see him but all could see the loot. His imprisoned heart pounded frantically on the bars of his ribs, his ears strained in expectation of shouts and curses. His shoulder muscles cringed in anticipation of impinging tearing bullets.

No warning yells followed him. No missiles slammed into his spine. The silence was worse than an uproar. He guessed, as he reached the door, that his feet had been faster than the onlookers' minds. He was making a successful getaway while they stood dumbfounded by the sight of a packet departing of its own volition.

He raced through the door like a charging bull, left it whirling behind him. Two hundred yards to the corner, another hundred to the junk-filled grating outside the pawnbroker's shop. If no snoopers were hanging around he could cache the money there and wander home at his leisure.

The hullabaloo started when he was within fifty yards of the corner. An excited mob poured out of the bank and saw the payroll bobbing fantastically above the pavement. Howls of *"Stop!"* roars of *"Get him!"* were followed by two sharp reports and a whine of lead above Mason's head.

Sprinting for the corner he almost collided with a pedestrian whose eyes bulged at the magically suspended package. Mason swung

an unseen but heavy fist to the fellow's jaw, and the man toppled to the ground. Shorty leaped over him and rounded the corner.

Eighty yards—forty—ten—separated him from the grating. He reached it a few seconds before his pursuers got to the corner. There were several people near but none had noticed the package; all were staring towards the junction from which came sounds of thudding feet and angry voices.

Mason bent, rammed the payroll between the side of the grating and the dusty window that ran down into the well. The package crimped, slid down, jammed again, then burst through. It flopped into the months'-old litter at the bottom of the well.

BENEATH the dull but broken sky the hunting pack swirled round the corner a full two hundred strong. They filled the narrow road from wall to wall, their numbers too great to evade.

Grinning to himself Mason raced up the road. A quick burst to the farther corner and he would reach the main avenue and lose the baying hounds for good. The money was safe, he was safe, the world was a wonderful place for guys who knew all the answers. Even Olympic champions didn't get forty thousand dollars for a quarter mile trot. The sun burst through the clouds, beaming in sympathy with his happiness.

Behind, the pack howled. Someone fired a shot and Mason heard the bullet moan across his shoulder. He increased his pace, still grinning. Let the fools shoot at random if it relieved their feelings.

Another shot, nearer this time. A hoarse command to halt. Mason, taking a hasty backward look, saw that the mob was gaining, They had passed the grating now and were less than fifty yards behind him with a uniformed policeman and the Legattrick bodyguard in the lead.

Even as Mason looked the policeman fired again. A hot iron seared the muscles of Mason's left arm and blood crept down to his wrist.

With nothing with which to wipe the blood away, he could only rush panting along, licking his arm as he ran. The corner came nearer—the mob came nearer, too. He was within ten yards of the busy main road when two policemen came running in from the other end. Leaping aside to avoid them, Mason gathered his muscles for the final effort which would carry him into obscurity and leave his pursuers foiled.

The policeman behind yelled something unintelligible, fired and cut a long red flake of brick from the wall at Mason's side.

Both of the policemen in front looked startled, snatched their guns and gestured toward Mason.

"Halt, you!" they shouted.

Desperately Mason dived for the gap between the opposing officers and the wall. Guns flamed on one side and from behind. Pain, red-hot, speared through him, stabbing his lungs. The force of the blows spun him around and, as he whirled, he knew that he was performing the pirouette of death.

He tottered off the sidewalk, bloody hands clasped to his abdomen, his shocked mind vaguely wondering how he, the unseen, could have been seen. How had anyone been able to aim at an invisible man? For two seconds he stood with glazing eyes turned toward the sun. Then, abruptly, he collapsed into the embrace of his own shadow—his treacherous shadow, which had been visible to others even though he himself was invisible!

THE END

AVON ONE SHOTS #1

COSMOS

CHAPTER 2
The Emigrants

By David H. Keller, M.D.

Matters were going from bad to worse on Earth. Even the most generous optimist secretly felt that the stage of mechanical labor had advanced to the point at which it might easily threaten the security, even the existence of the human race.

The robot had been followed by the super automaton. Machinery could now be so delicately attuned to the nervous system of mankind that all that was necessary was to develop the power of physic control, buy a few machines and let them work for their master. Naturally, the man who could buy the most machines and learn how to govern them was able to subdue the poor man who could only boast of a few imperfect automatons of early vintage.

At first only the visionaries thought of the possibility of a time's arriving when the automatons would function without the aid of a guiding human intelligence. But that time came. Almost before the human race were aware of their danger they were placed in a position of it's being hard to tell whether the intelligence of man was directing the activities of the machine or the intelligence of the machine was gradually enslaving the remnant of the human species.

James Tarvish, old, shrewd, wealthy, realized before most of the world's rich men what might happen on the earth. Having neither wife nor child, he had made money his God, and machinery his hobby. It was his cash which made the dream of interplanetary travel become a living reality. Though not an inventor himself, he was able to tell the men under his rule what to invent. Silently, vigorously, relentlessly he fought the battle against the automatons, but finally realized the fact that it might easily become a hopeless fight. Five years before the two great forces came into open conflict he had made up his mind what to do. Once he decided he worked with startling rapidity.

He called in his inventors and scientists from all parts of the world. When he talked to them his words snapped, his sentences crackled.

"Draw plans for two air-ships that will fit together to form one interplanetary ship. I want them so designed that the two can be used independently or, when joined in the middle, can be used as one. Double everything. Make it powerful, swift, the finest ship ever made. In the one ship I want a giant refrigerator built. In fact, I want the entire half to be a refrigerator. Think of the greatest heat possible, the most terrible heat known to our intelligence and then plan a refrigerating plant that will enable a human being to live inside no matter what the heat is outside, and keep on living there, year after year. You have broken up the atom to obtain energy. Learn how to use that energy to produce cold. Stock both ends of the ship with everything necessary to keep several people alive for many years; not only alive, but happy and busy and interested in life.

"I am not taking anything for impossible. I know what I want and I want it right and as fast as possible. Spare no expense. Put yourself on double hours of labor and triple units of salary. Get busy and stay busy. I am going to be on the job day and night. If you are not sure of what I want, ask me. If you are not sure you can do what I want get out and give a better man the job."

"Where are you going in this ship, Mr. Tarvish?" asked one of the best minds in the gathering. "We ought to know that in order to design it properly."

"You build it the way I say," was the sharp answer, "and it will go where it is intended to go. If I had wanted to tell you my plans I would have done so at once."

The rocket-ship was built. As a mechanical triumph it was a success. As a novelty in interplanetary travel it was filled with startling new innovations.

Tarvish had used the very mechanical perfection that he was

afraid of to devise a space home that was in everyway foolproof. Anyone knowing enough to read and press buttons could guide the machine through the void of time and space and live in it for the full span of individual existence.

In two years it was built.

Known among the inventors as Fool's Folly and called by the fictionists the Ark of Space, it contained something that was more remarkable than any part of its automatic machinery. It held an idea. James Tarvish, old, dour, canny, tightfisted, had an idea and it was a new one.

For the next three months he hunted for a man.

He wanted a man who was brave, intellectual, clean, and in every way representative of the best in the cultural achievements of the age. He at last found what he wanted. The man's name was Henry Cecil.

"I have a job for you, Mr. Cecil," whispered Tarvish.

"I accept it," was the sharp reply.

"But you don't know what it is?"

"And I do not care, as long as I can support myself."

"You can do that if you take this job. I have built a space-ship. I want you to be the entire crew. I am sending you away from the world— forever."

"How about my pay?"

"I will have a number of envelopes filled, each with the salary for one month. On the first of each month you can open an envelope."

"That's satisfactory. On a trip of

that kind I ought to be able to save a lot."

"A lot! Man! You can save it all. I wish I had had a chance like that when I was a lad. Here is the idea. The world is going to smash. I do not mean physically, but socially. The automatons are gaining in power. The day will come when they will either kill or enslave what is left of the human race. I want to save what is best of it so I am sending out this space-ship. It is the Ark that will save mankind from the second deluge, the flood of mechanical perfection."

"And I am going to send you to a place that is safe. An ordinary space-ship cannot follow you. You will be safe."

"All by myself?"

"Practically. Perhaps a pet for you to talk to."

"It is ideal!" cried the young man eagerly. "Wonderful! In fact, is just what I have been hunting for. No women?"

The old man frowned.

"Women! And me a bachelor all my life? I said I wanted to save the best of our culture, not the dregs."

"You don't like women?"

"No, when I was young one woman called me a dried-out orange, a book that had been read, a worn-out shoe. She intimated that the masculine sex was the inferior one. I have not liked women since that day. And you!"

"That is one reason I want to take this job. There is a woman after me. She thinks that she would like to marry me. So long as I am on this Earth I cannot escape her. So, I am leaving."

"Young? Pretty? Healthy? Intelligent?"

"Sure. All of that, but she treats me as if I were a child. She wants to make plans for me, buy my neckties, and all that sort of thing."

"You poor lad. Tell me her name and address and I will see that you are protected. What kind of a pet will be your choice?"

"An English bull dog. I will get a puppy."

"Better get one that is housebroke. There will be no pleasant fields where you are going."

"Just where is my future home?"

"Mercury. It is the only place that the automatons will not think of conquering."

"But it is hot there. Near the sun and all that sort of thing."

"Sure it is hot, but you will be living in a refrigerator, with goldfish in the aquarium and canaries in the bird cage. So long as you stay in the refrigerator, you will be safe. A second outside and you will be a cinder."

"Fine! Even if the temperature is high it will not be as hot as a life with Ruth Fanning. That is the girl's name. I will write her address for you. When do I go?"

"In a week. I may not be there to see you off, but all you have to do is to follow your written orders. The salary is a hundred a month for your life, payable on the first of each month."

The young man seized the old man's hand. His appreciation was pathetic, as he exclaimed, "I never shall be able to thank you for this. If the offer had not come, that girl would have caught me in another month. Now I shall go out and hunt up that bulldog. What did you say the object of the trip was?"

"To save humanity. To preserve the human race."

"That is some job for the bulldog and me, but we shall do our best. I am going to show you that you have not made a mistake in selecting me. Just why did you do it?"

"Because I found out that you are a misogynist."

"I see. And you will take care of Ruth?"

"You just leave that to me."

"O.K."

* * * * *

Most of the following week was devoted to the mechanical education of Henry Cecil. Hour after hour he was taught how to push the various buttons and find his way through space. He was shown all the parts of the super-refrigeration machinery. He was not an engineer; in fact, he was simply an author, but at the end of the week he felt that he would be able to do everything that was necessary on the trip, which was to occupy his lifetime.

The day came! The hour! The minute! He said goodbye to the men who had tutored him and, as the bulldog barked, he shut and fastened the door, and pushed the various buttons that started the giant ship on its journey to one of the infernos of the universe.

Mercury! The planet nearest the sun. The planet of mystery, of terrible heat, the place human life is supposed to be impossible. The place even a determined young lady could not follow a man she coveted.

The bulldog, slightly uneasy at what he could not understand, whined at Cecil's feet. He looked out of a window, and through the heavy insulated glass and peered at the disappearing Earth. The man bent over and pulled the dog's ears.

"Alone at last, old man," he cried. "Just you and me, and the world of woman left behind. Suppose we go into the library?"

In that room, above the murmur of the machinery, he heard a rhythmic snore. He walked rapidly to the chair. The old man woke.

"Why, Mr. Tarvish!" cried Cecil. "What are you doing there in that chair?"

"I must have overslept," chuckled the gray-headed man. "Came in here at the last moment to look around and got sleepy. Well, since I am paying the cost for the saving of the human race, I might as well witness the details of the salvaging. It will be a grand adventure, Henry, and I doubt not we shall never regret it. I have a surprise for you. When I came on the ship my dog followed me. As fine an English bull as you ever saw, and a bitch."

"What?"

"Sure! Dogs die. They wither and grow old and die. We will live on and

what would life be without a dog? Why, man, the human race has always had dogs; so, when you told me what kind of a dog you were going to take, I went and got a mate for him."

"And you intended to make the trip with me all the time?"

"A suspicious person might think so."

Just then the door opened. A young woman walked in. She was young and beautiful and she looked as though she might be intellectual. She wore a pretty little apron and she smiled as she asked, "What time shall you men want supper?"

"At five, my dear, and I like my toast a trifle hard, with orange marmalade and tea."

As the woman left the room, Cecil turned on the old man.

"So, you did that to me? After all your fine words about being a woman hater, and selecting me because you knew I was a misogynist, and all that sort of thing, you go and take her with us."

"Now don't take it too hard," advised Tarvish.

"It really was on account of the dogs I did it," he added.

"What had the dogs to dogs to do with your allowing Ruth to come?"

"'Twas like this. There will be little puppies, Henry, and you know what a little pup is like. One of the things it likes to do more than anything else is to play with a baby. Now, we cannot be cruel to the little dog and deprive it of its happiness."

"How about me? Are you

comparing my happiness to that of a dog?"

"Not exactly; but look here. You are on a salary. One hundred a week for the rest of your life. You are hired to save humanity. That is your job, and how can you save it without a woman?"

"I do not want the job. Not if it means what it seems to mean."

The old scientist shook his head, "I do not know what you are talking about. I thought I was doing you a favor. It seemed to me that a lifetime in a refrigerator would be tiresome, and you would tire of playing cribbage with me. Besides, there is the matter of toast. I like it just a certain way, and if it is any other way the meal is spoiled. Ruth knows how to toast it so it is just right. She has made me toast at irregular intervals for years. You will be surprised to learn that she is my favorite niece. Another thing; the trip was her idea. She suggested it. My first thought was that she and I would make the trip by ourselves, but she felt that you needed a change; that you were too closely confined at your job. So, I had you come along to please her. It seems to me that the more I try to help people the more I am misunderstood."

"I'll be damned!" exclaimed Cecil.

"You probably will unless you make an effort to be nice to Ruth. She said your excuse for not marrying her was the lack of a sufficient income and enough leisure. You have both now. Suppose we have supper."

*　*　*　*　*

Hours passed and days. Weeks folded up their tired frames and went to sleep in the cemetery of time. The old man spent more and more time in the library, usually with one or both bulldogs. Cecil learned to be nice to Ruth. They found that, given leisure and an adequate income, they had a number of things in common.

At last they reached Mercury and landed on its superheated surface. In every way the refrigerating mechanicism worked as it was supposed to work. Life in the space-ship was pleasant, placid and peaceful. The bullpups were growing up. Ruth and Cecil were growing up. The old man laughed more and more to himself.

Over the space radio they received news from the Earth. It was not at all pleasant and confirmed Travish's worst anticipations. The automatons were winning the struggle for supremacy. Unless something happened the human race would be enslaved and then destroyed.

Tarvish laughed over these messages and commented, "At least, we have made Mercury safe for humanity."

"And for the race of bulldogs," added Ruth, running into the room. "Our population is increased by four of the finest little pups you ever saw." She rushed out as fast as she had rushed in.

"Poor little doggies!" sighed Tarvish, looking at the young man out of one corner of his eye. "No babies for them to play with."

"Ruth is looking after that," replied Cecil rather sadly.

"She is a great girl," purred the old man. "Wait a minute, are you two married?"

"Yes. The night before I left the Earth I consented to a formal marriage. I had not told her of my plans to take this trip and spend the rest of my life away from Earth, so, just to please her, I let her have her way and we were married. I said goodbye to her at the church, never expecting to see her again, and all the time she knew she was going to make the space trip with me. I do not believe I ever will trust a woman again. It has been a wonderful lesson to me."

"How do you like her cooking?"
Cecil brightened up.

"Keep your clothes in order."

Cecil beamed. The old man smiled as he whispered, "Let's play a game of cribbage, you confirmed misogynist."

*   *   *   *   *

A month later the little doggies had two babies to play with, twins, a boy and a girl. It began to look as though a start was made toward the saving of humanity.

And then the mysterious message came to them.

For three days all Earth messages over the super radio were blocked. Evidently some supreme power was preventing all radio waves in order to clear the ether for its own purposes. Then the message came over and over again as though in fear that if only sent one time or a dozen times it would be lost.

People of Mercury: Construct a space-ship in accord with our instructions which will follow and send a representative to the crater Copernicus of the satellite of the third planet.

Signed: Dos-Tev

Tarvish thought it over from every possible viewpoint. At last he called Henry Cecil into the library and told him to shut the door.

"What do you think about it, Henry?" he asked.

"Ruth says that Henry, Jr., gained a half pound last week, but cries a good deal. Little Angelica laughs a goo-goo laugh, but does not grow as fast as her brother."

The old man looked disgusted.

"Being a father ruined you as a general conversationalist. All you can talk about is babies, babies, babies. Henry, Jr., is probably crying because he has found out that he is a male, and Angelica say goo-goo because she belongs to the superior sex. What I want to know is your opinion of the message we have been receiving."

"Oh! That? What I do not understand is how they knew we came to Mercury?"

"They don't know. They just hoped there was some form of life on Mercury and wanted to communicate with it. But why?"

"Perhaps they are having an interplanetary Rotarian Meeting of some sort and want us to send representatives?"

"That is a silly thought, Henry, but there may be something to it. They may be sending the same message to every planet, and the message we received is the same the people received on earth. It may be a grand hoax and then again it may be something very vital, something so great in its scope that even a limited comprehension of it is impossible. But I have made up my mind as to what to do. I am going to separate the two parts of our ship, leave you and Ruth and the babies here with some of the dogs and I am going to take the other half of the ship and go to the Moon and find out what it all means."

"You are going to do nothing of the kind!" declared a very convincing and determined voice.

"Ruth Cecil! Do you mean to tell me you have been listening?"

"How could I help it?" replied the young mother. "I come in here to ask you for advice in regard to the children and find you making plans to go off and leave us here. I am not going to let you!"

"You better let us settle this, Ruth," urged the old man.

"Certainly; he knows best," added Cecil. "It is no trip for babies to make."

"Have it your own way," replied the defeated girl. "What do you want for supper?"

* * * * *

That night Tarvish dreamed he was floating through space. There was a slight sense of nausea, a deeper sense of impending danger. The room seemed chilled. He awoke, shivered, felt the unusual vibration of some powerful machinery. Startled, he jumped out of bed, pulled on a dressing robe and ran into the adjoining bedroom. Cecil was in bed, still asleep, but sneezing. The babies were well covered, as were the dogs. Ruth was missing.

"Where's Ruth?" asked Tarvish, shaking Cecil by the shoulder.

The young man awoke, looked around, collected himself and gasped, "Gone."

They ran through the half of the ship which had served them for a home on Mercury. The woman was not to be found. Looking out the windows, they learned part of the truth. The ship had left Mercury and the hot planet was already receding. An open door told the rest of the tale.

Startled beyond words, they ran into the other end of the space-ship and found Ruth in the control room, busily engaged in pressing buttons and studying a map of the universe.

She was the only calm one of the three.

"What are you doing, Ruth?" demanded the old man.

"I have started this family to the Moon."

"But who said you should?" asked the husband.

"I said so, silly boy. Do you think we were going to stay in that dull inferno and let Uncle make the trip by himself? Once he was gone, what was to happen to us? And our children? All well enough to talk about saving Mercury for humanity, but we brought children into the world, and, if we stay on Mercury whom would they marry? And where would they go to school? I want them to have a little social life. And then we have to consider their collegiate education. And how about the dogs? Two of the little pups are females. They ought to have their chance. And then there are other things. Who would make Uncle's toast for him if I did not stay with him? And I am out of the yellow floss for my hooked rug and cannot do a thing on it till I get some more, and you need some new stockings, and my watch does not keep time, and next year is the fifth reunion of my class and all of the Sorority will be back and they will expect me there. I am the Grand Historian. So, we are all going to the moon, and after that we are going back to New York and do some shopping, and I wish you would find out which button to press to turn on the heat, because now that we are away from Mercury we have nothing to neutralize the cold of the refrigerating system; and if you men feel the way I do, you are not at all comfortable. I covered the babies up before I left them, but I suppose they are uncovered by this time; so, I am going back to look after them and leave you men with the machinery. I set the course for the moon, but just at this minute I feel that perhaps I looked on the wrong page and we are now heading for Mars instead. You see, they both start with M, and it is confusing. Goodnight. See you at breakfast."

"Wonderful girl!" sighed the old man. "College graduate."

"She is wonderful," agreed the young man. "At times when I am with her I feel like killing her, yet, when I am away from her for just a few minutes I feel so lonely I know I could not live without her. Did you ever feel that way about a woman?"

The old man did not answer the question. Cecil continued, "Did you listen to her stream of thought? Was it logical? Was it connected? Was there any sense to it?"

"Women don't think as men do," sighed Tarvish.

"I wonder if they think at all!"

The correct adjustments were made to the machinery. Gradually the ship grew more comfortable. Looking out through the windows, the two men saw Mercury, now simply a pin point of super-heated metal. One of the bulldogs ran in, sat down at the old man's feet, and started to lick his hand. Far in the distance they heard the laugh of a little baby.

"We are going to the Moon," said the old man, "for new adventures, but it is nice to think that no matter what happens to us we are going as a family, all of us, even the little doggies."

Ruth called in through the door.

"What do you men want for breakfast?"

The ship sped speedily spaceward.

TO BE CONTINUED

Don't Miss Any Of Our Magazines!

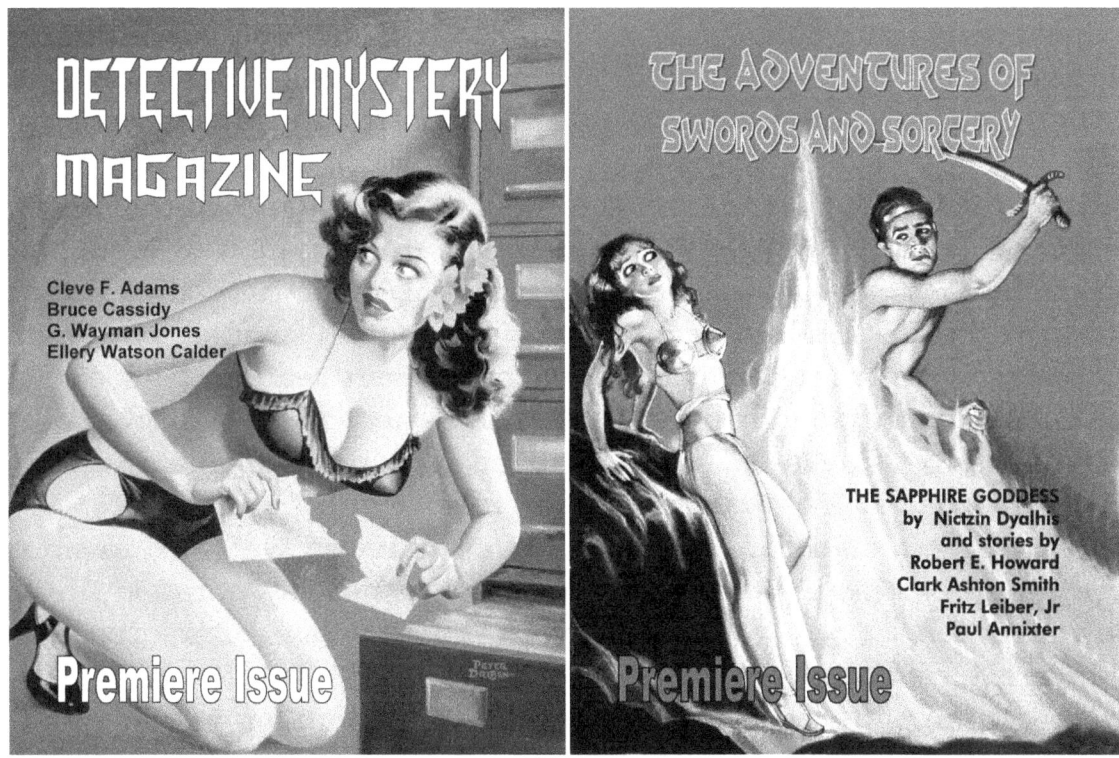

TREASURES OF TANTALUS

By Garret Smith

Part Two

CHAPTER X
The Larceny Section in Action

FROM now on we began gradually to find the trust operations less bewildering. By constant study of the various guarded communications between members and listening in at Judge Tanner's council meetings, we came to catch the drift of the organization's political plans and eventually to understand the code they used when discussing particularly delicate matters.

In the coming Congress, the members were divided by the trust manipulators into those who could be controlled already, those who could be relied on to favor naturally the trust proposals, and those who would oppose them from conviction and could be won only by argument or indirect methods. As it stood, Chandler thus had a bare working majority, but had elaborate plans for increasing his margin before the session was over.

No violently revolutionary measures were contemplated at the outset. They were to begin with slight and apparently harmless revisions of the laws that had hampered the predatory business interests in re-cent years, inserting unsuspected jokers that would make secret violations easier and conviction more difficult. This was to be followed by a campaign of insidious propaganda that would eventually make the popular will lenient to a complete repealing of those cramping laws.

In the more narrowly criminal direction they aimed at liberalizing the laws governing the release of inmates of detention farms. They also had planned an elaborate campaign for gradually filling the courts of every degree with judges under control of the trust.

In short, the nation at large was under the complete rule of a criminal oligarchy which was about to plunder it so artfully that the complacent public would pay tribute without even realizing its exploitation. It was not till now that we realized fully the extreme difficulty of the task of exposure.

Nevertheless we were in no way daunted. Priestley pursued the task with all the zeal of a crusader of old. I found his enthusiasm contagious. What emotions were at play behind the green eyeshade of the taciturn Miss Stimson, Professor Fleckner's able and conscientious secretary, I could only guess, but I

noted that she watched every move of Priestley with her shy, sidewise glance, and was quick to second any suggestion of his.

As for Fleckner himself, his demeanor became colder and more impersonal as our investigation proceeded. It was more and more evident to me at this time that his interest in the whole affair began and ended in his hope of finding the hiding place of the Treasures of Tantalus. But for a time we made no more progress in this direction.

Then, a little over a month after our last fiasco, we ran again upon a warm trail.

During one of Judge Tanner's council meetings we got the first hint that the larceny section of the crime trust was about to go into action after a long period of quiet. The judge had called up Chandler as usual to give his report and receive instructions.

"And now," came the hoarse whisper of the Voice Higher Up, "your boys below can indulge in a little fun again. We need two. No publicity this time."

"All right," the judge agreed, "the section has been working up some good prospects. I think they can do it in one job."

Chandler hung up and Tanner twisted the ring connecting with the underground rendezvous.

"Give me 72," he directed, and presently he was talking with a short, thick-set fellow whose face under the black mask might have been that of a boss plumber.

"We want two this time," the judge directed. "Can you do it in one job and no publicity?"

"I can," the other answered promptly. "I have a plant all laid. Can finish it in about two weeks."

"Very good, go at it immediately."

The judge hung up and returned to his companions at the table.

For your information," he said to Winter, "I will explain that two million dollars is about to be added to the organization's reserve fund out of the vaults of one of our leading banks, and the deed will be accomplished so that the chances are the officers of the bank will never discover their loss."

"But how? I don't understand!" Winter exclaimed.

"That's all I can tell you, because that's all I know," the judge replied. "That's all I want to know. Remember what I said about curiosity. If by any chance I happened to learn more than that I would be no more immune to deadly disease or a sud-

den accident than were the two misguided gentlemen I've told you about."

Meantime we were following the movements of No. 72, whom Tanner had just been instructing. He walked swiftly through the crowd and singled out two other black-robed, masked figures. Nos. 116 and 297, touching an elbow of each as he passed. He went on into one of the little conference-rooms off the main clubroom, and within a few minutes the two he had signalled casually joined him and closed the door.

"The big job is on," No. 72 announced. "Is the fake stuff ready?"

"I'll have it in the warehouse on twelve hours' notice," replied No. 116.

"Can you start the digging tonight?" No. 72 asked No. 297.

"Within two hours. I've kept the van there with tools and plenty of room for the dirt."

"All right, go to it," No. 72 approved. "Give No. 116 the word when the job's within twelve hours of finished."

"We can make it about Friday night," No. 297 decided as he went out.

We kept this digger gentleman on the screen and immediately began watching interesting developments.

He strolled about the main room for a few moments, now and then casually jogging an elbow of one of the company, until he had thus served secret notice on six of his fellow members. Each man summoned, withdrew unostentatiously, and presently all six were out on the street in ordinary citizens' clothes. They paid no attention to each other, but apparently departed on their various ways bound for home.

They were all well-dressed, presentable-looking young chaps, having the appearance of students or young professional men. A little later they were followed by No. 297, an older man who looked like a prosperous contractor. He proceeded to the parking plaza in front of the Riccadona, got into a high-powered limousine and turned south.

A little way down the avenue he directed the chauffeur suddenly to the curb and hailed a gentleman who was sauntering along in the same direction.

"Hello, John!" he called genially, swinging open the car door, "let me give you a lift."

"Don't care if I do; thanks," replied the other, looking up in apparent surprise and then seeming to recognize a friend.

He was one of the six helpers who had left the underground club after being nudged by No. 297.

The car turned at the next corner and swung around a block, until the owner, peering out the rear window, seemed assured that no one was following. Then they turned back into the avenue, and a block below picked up another of the six helpers. This was repeated until the six were all aboard.

About 1 A. M. they crossed 125th Street in Seventh Avenue on the upper street level, which as usual was practically deserted at that time of night. On the southwest corner stood in those days the huge pile of the Great International Trust Company, and when the limousine swung into 124th Street, back of this building, we guessed at once that this was the robbers' objective point.

Across the street from the trust company building was the dark pyramidal pile of a storage warehouse. Next it was an old transient hotel that still clung to the down-town district. A one-story arcade automobile entrance thrust itself between the wall of the warehouse and that story of the hotel. Into this the car turned and stopped in front of the hotel entrance.

One of No. 297's helpers descended from the the car as a sleepy doorman emerged from the hotel. Simultaneously the leader and his five assistants, unseen by the doorman, alighted on the other side of the car and stood hidden by the car body. The man who had got out at the hotel entrance handed his bag to the doorman and turned to the chauffeur.

"Wait till I get some change at the desk," he said, and went in with the doorman.

The moment the hotel door closed the leader of the digger gang reached into the car again, drew out another suit-case, opened it, and revealed a small high-power blow-flame apparatus. Over the flame nozzle he placed a concealing hood of asbestos, and then, keeping in the shadow of the automobile, went over to a window of the storage warehouse that was protected by heavy steel bars set deep into the concrete wall.

Against the concrete about the end of a bar he directed the nozzle and turned on the flame. In a moment the setting of the bar was as loose as any sand. Repeating the process at the other end of the bar, he was presently able to wrench it free. By the time the man who had gone into the hotel returned with his change, three bars had been removed, the heavy window and iron shutters behind them jimmied open, and five men had crept through into the darkness beyond. No. 297 waited until the sixth man had returned from the hotel, then whistling a soft signal to him, crept into the warehouse after his men.

The outside man went around the car to the breached window, put the bars back in place, plastered some new soft concrete back about their ends with a trowel from the car's tool-box, smoothed it down, hid the marks with a little paint from a patent paint-tube, returned the tools, and after a whispered word to the chauffeur, went back into the hotel and to the room he had engaged for the night. His part of the job was evidently over. He retired immediately and was snoring five minutes later.

Meantime No. 297, within the warehouse, taking a new window lock from his tool-kit, replaced the one he had broken and concealed the marks with a paint-tube. Then the six men tiptoed silently through the great building until they heard a watchman coming on his rounds.

Concealing his men down a side passage, No. 297 hid behind a pillar to which was attached one of the automatic sentry-clocks whose button the watchman was due to punch once an hour. As the watchman approached the clock the hidden crook drew a small spraying bulb from his pocket, held his breath, and sprayed a fine invisible vapor in the watchman's face.

At first it seemed to have no effect. The man punched the button and went on his rounds. But his steps grew slower and heavier as he went. He reached the little office where he sat between rounds, threw himself in his chair, and a moment later was sprawled over his desk fast asleep.

In less than fifteen minutes' time they had in this way put out of commission for the night the watchmen on each floor. What these fellows thought on awaking the next morning we had no means of knowing and no time to speculate regarding it. As one of the gang of crooks attended to punching the time-clock so that there would be no interruption from the district police station where the hourly reports registered, it is to be presumed that each watchman thought that he was the only derelict, and that a friendly brother watchman had discovered his plight and attended to his record. Naturally he dared ask no questions.

At any rate the moment the last watchman was asleep the diggers hurried to a big van stored with others on the main floor, drove it on one of the elevators, and descended to the sub-basement. They backed the van out of the elevator and over to a point near the front foundation wall of the building.

They worked now with the speed of careful rehearsal. No. 297 snatched from the van another blow-flame apparatus similar to that used in entering the building and burned a deep groove about a four foot square of the concrete flooring. Then a small electric crane was extended from the rear of the van and this block of flooring was lifted out and set aside.

Next a rotary electric earth and rock drill with a four-foot bore was hoisted down over this opening and attached to the light cable. From it into the van was stretched a jointed extension chute through which the detritus from the drill was dumped into the van.

When they stopped work just before daybreak the big van was nearly full of earth and ground rock, and a four-foot tunnel extended down under the foundation wall and several feet under the street toward the Trust Company building.

They stowed the apparatus out of sight in the tunnel, sealed up the opening, ran the van back to its place up-stairs, climbed in on top of the pile of earth, and after eating sandwiches from a hamper under the seat, calmly went to sleep.

About nine o'clock in the morning a driver presented himself at the warehouse office with proper credentials and took the van away. An hour later the contents were dumped in a lonely stream in the Putnam County Forest Reserve.

In the afternoon another van came in and put up for the night. As soon as the day force left, No. 297 and his five helpers emerged from the van and went to work again. To our surprise they paid no attention to the watchman. We were puzzled until we noted that the personnel of the watchmen had entirely changed. The all-powerful trust had evidently substituted its own men.

The work of boring the tunnel across the street and up under the vault of the Trust Company was completed in this way in less than the week set for the job. The day before the night appointed for the grand coup, word was passed through the regular channels, and, on order for a special grade of cotton, a van-load of counterfeit gold and paper money wrapped in cotton bolts, to the amount of two million dollars, came down from the Fall River counterfeiting plant under the cotton mill, and was stored in the 124th Street warehouse.

That night No. 116 and a group

of helpers emerged from hiding in this van, unsealed the tunnel, carried the counterfeit millions through to the Trust Company vault and substituted them for their equivalent in real money, which they brought back and stored in the van.

The next day the trust company did business as usual, its officers never dreaming that two million dollars in worthless imitation money rested in its vaults, and that some of this spurious specie passed out of its windows to customers.

Meantime, late in the afternoon, the van with its burden of real wealth rumbled across the northern city line into the Putnam County hills, headed toward the secret hiding-place of the Treasures of Tantalus.

CHAPTER XI
A Treasure Astray

MEANTIME we watched with acute interest the forging of the link by which the treasure was to pass from these outside workers, who blindly obeyed orders, to Chandler, who alone knew the final hiding-place of the trust's reserve fund. And this must be accomplished without the identity of the custodian becoming known to even the most trusted of his henchmen.

The night before the getaway from the warehouse, Judge Tanner dined in the little room at the Riccadona. He received word from No.

72 over the wall phone that all would be ready the following night, and got back from Chandler the cryptic order:

"Eleven at point twenty."

Tanner passed this back to No. 72. This we took to mean that the money would be transferred at eleven o'clock at night at a point designated as No. 20 on the secret chart of the trust.

The following afternoon Chandler and his family ran out to their country-place for the night. About nine o'clock the president-elect bade them good night.

"I've got a speech to prepare, and I'm going to work it out on a midnight tramp," he remarked as he left the room.

Mrs. Chandler laughed indulgently.

"I wonder if your father really thinks better while he's tramping or only imagines it," she remarked to her daughter.

"I don't know," the girl answered. "I should think he'd get all fagged out. He didn't get back till after three o'clock the last time he had one of his tramp sessions. I was awake with a headache that night and heard him come in."

Meanwhile Chandler, protected from the crisp air by heavy furs, was swinging rapidly along the narrow, lonely country road that skirted the high iron fence around his estate. At a point in the woodland about a mile from the entrance to the grounds, he stopped and searched the fence for a little distance with a flash-light. After a moment he reached down, found a secret spring, pressed it, and swung open a section of the fence a dozen feet wide. He entered and dived under the thick underbrush for a few rods.

Reaching a little tree-enclosed clearing, he searched the trunks of the trees about its margin with his light and then pressed against a knot on one of them. Immediately a little clump of huckleberry bushes in the center of the clearing began to rise up from the ground supported on four small steel columns. We heard the hum of underground machinery. At the height of about six feet the platform of earth and shrubbery stopped, revealing the opening into a cavern of considerable size, lined with concrete.

"The hiding place of our Treasures of Tantalus!" Priestley exclaimed.

"Oh, it can't be! It can't be!" Miss Stimson cried out, and then shrank back, abashed at her sudden vehemence.

Fleckner looked at her sharply.

"Why not?" he demanded.

"He would hardly run the risk of having it connected so closely with himself," I interposed, coming to the embarrassed girl's rescue, but a little surprised at her sudden forwardness.

"Possibly not." Fleckner conceded reluctantly, "but I'm going to find out."

He ran the telephonoscope ray all about the underground chamber, but discovered nothing except three small collapsible airplanes. He pierced the walls with the ray at all points, but everywhere it ran into solid earth.

He stopped, baffled, just as Chandler was dragging forth one of the planes.

"It's simply a place to store machines for secret flights," he decided. "He's on his way to meet the treasure van."

With the machine outside, Chandler closed the hidden hangar and dragged the plane out to the road, shutting the secret gate after him. In less than twenty minutes after he left the house he was high above the clouds, speeding at three hundred and fifty miles an hour toward the Putnam County hills into which, on another section of our screen, we were watching the treasure van advance.

A few minutes later, nearly a hundred miles from his starting point, he settled down in a country road hidden by heavy woods, only about a half a mile ahead of the oncoming van. He alighted, drew his machine off the road, and then proceeded to make a lightning change. He drew off his outer garments and hid them in the machine's cockpit. Three minutes later he stood in an ordinary freight-van driver's uniform, his complexion altered with a few touches from a make-up outfit by the aid of his flash and a small mirror, a heavy false mustache drooping over the lower part of his face, and his cap well over his eyes.

He had barely completed his transformation when the van rumbled up to within a hundred yards of where he stood. Then suddenly the engine went dead. The driver manipulated its levers and the machine back-fired sharply three times, and then after a brief interval twice more and was silent.

This, it appeared, was a signal, for Chandler answered with a single, long-drawn-out cry of a wildcat. At that the van-driver went to the back of the van and drew out a folded airplane similar to the one in which Chandler had come, unfolded it, and the next moment, with muffled motor and darkened lamps, soared silently into the air and away. Chandler, trundling his own plane ahead of him, was approaching the van.

"Ah!" whispered Fleckner exultantly. "He is at last about to lead us to the treasure-trove!"

I heard a sharp gasp behind me, and turning, looked squarely, for the first time, I think, into the eyes of Professor Fleckner's secretary. I remember being surprised to note that they were fine eyes, of deep violet hue.

Her green shade was awry for once, but she had forgotten it. She seemed unaware that I was looking at her. She was staring in terror at the figure of Chandler as he approached the van, and the moment when he would unwittingly become the instrument of his own undoing. She clasped and unclasped her hands convulsively.

I looked again at the screen. Chandler had reached the van and was preparing to put his plane aboard. Fleckner and Priestley stood with eyes glued on the screen, hardly breathing. It was as though they feared that the slightest sound in the laboratory half a hundred miles away might frighten the head of the crime trust from his purpose and break again the thread that was leading us to his secret. Neither of them, I am sure, had noted the girl's little byplay.

I heard a half-sob behind me. I turned toward the girl again. She stood with tears running down her face, her hands stretched out toward Fleckner imploringly. She swayed as if faint, and clutched at the control board near her for support.

"Oh, don't! Don't!" she cried hysterically.

I heard a smothered exclamation from Fleckner as he sprang for the control board. Then, for the first time, I realized that Miss Stimson, when she clutched the board, had hit and thrown over the projection-lever. I was right in the line of projection. I whirled around just in time to see my own image on the screen projected out there in the Putnam County woods beside the head of the crime trust.

He, too, had seen me and heard the girl's warning cry, for he was climbing aboard his airplane in a panic. His back was toward me when I turned, and I hoped he had not seen my face. He unfolded his wings and threw on the power in the same instant. The next instant the President-elect of these United States fled, a panic-stricken criminal, leaving two million dollars in stolen money out in that wintry woodland.

Fleckner was beside himself with rage. He stormed about the laboratory, hurling abuses on the head of the girl, who had slipped to the floor in a faint and was mercifully unable to hear. Priestley and I carried her to a lounge, and he held a bottle of restorative to her nostrils.

The moment she began to show signs of returning consciousness, Fleckner stood over her and began to redouble his abuse. Thereupon Priestley turned upon him in a cold rage. He clenched his fists threateningly.

"Not another word," he commanded. "If I hear another bit of abuse from you, old a man as you are, I'll knock you down. This poor girl has been taken with sudden illness. Do you think she did it purposely?"

Fleckner stated at him, speechless with rage, for an instant. Then he started to speak, but what he saw in the younger man's blazing eyes halted him.

He turned back to the screen without another word.

Miss Stimson opened her eyes and suddenly realized that her eyeshade no longer sheltered them. With a frightened little gesture she readjusted it. Then, after a moment she got up, apologized for making us trouble, and said she would better go home as she felt ill.

Fleckner was intently studying the screen and hardly noted her departure.

"Poor little thing!" Priestley exclaimed. "She's been overworking here lately and is nervously exhausted."

"Humph!" the professor grunted. "She might better have stayed away to-night. I'm afraid neither Chandler nor any of his gang will dare recover that treasure-van and go on. They'll not take the slightest risk of discovery. We've lost our chance of tracing the treasure-trove for the present. I'd discharge that bungling girl for what she did if she weren't so generally valuable."

Priestley glared at him, but said nothing.

For myself I was not lacking in sympathy for the young woman's distress, particularly after my glimpse into those disturbing violet eyes, but I also had misgivings about her when I recalled her agitation just before the final catastrophe. I couldn't help wondering whether the throwing on of the projection lever was altogether accidental, but I kept my suspicions to myself, and presently the events that were being pictured on the screen drove them out of my mind.

Chandler was plainly in a panic for fear of discovery. He rose straight into the air about three miles after the sudden alarm, then shot off for fifty miles or so in a direction opposite to his New Jersey place, listening constantly in his wireless detector to see if any other plane was pursuing. Finally, apparently satisfied, he swung back in a wide circle, and an hour later arrived at the secret hangar on his estate, put up his plane, removed his disguise, and a few minutes later rang the front doorbell at his house. It was then only one o'clock.

"Sorry to trouble you," he said to the sleepy servant who admitted him. "I found I'd left my keys in my other clothes."

"Good Lord!" he added, looking at his watch. "It's one o'clock!"

This we took to be for purposes of alibi.

In his room he began to pace the floor nervously. He looked worn and haggard with worry. We could imagine his predicament. He had no idea who could be the strange man who interrupted him as he was about to take possession of the treasure. He could not guess how much that man knew. Perhaps he, President-elect of the United States, was facing exposure on the morrow. He dared not go back to the van or send any of his lieutenants there. No knowing what ambush might await them.

Several times he paused in his nervous pacing and looked speculatively at the telephone. But he shook his head despairingly at last.

"Nobody I dare reach, and nothing they could do if I did," he muttered.

Apparently in this unlooked for emergency was betrayed a weak spot in the trust system. He had not dared let any one assist him in final disposal of the treasure, and no one but he now knew of his failure.

He stopped suddenly and stood with clenched fists, a look of new rage on his face.

"There's a traitor in camp!" he exclaimed aloud.

Meantime the van stood silent and unmolested on the deserted forest road. After we had watched this lifeless spectacle, and the almost equally monotonous one of Chandler futilely pacing his bedchamber for upwards of an hour, we grew weary of inaction. We were all three of us tired and irritable from excitement, disappointment and lack of sleep.

Out of this situation grew a lively wrangle between Priestley and Professor Fleckner. Priestley ventured the suggestion that we take steps to restore the stolen money to the trust company, now that the chance of its leading us to the main treasure had passed.

Fleckner sneered openly at this.

"How would you go about it without exposing our method of getting it and thus ending our hope of destroying the system, as well as exposing ourselves to its punishment?" he asked after they had disputed hotly over the ethics involved.

"This gives us pretty tangible evidence against the crime trust, doesn't it?" Priestley demanded.

"Nothing that would trap Chandler or even Tanner," Fleckner insisted.

Priestley argued this point at some length, but was fair enough to admit finally that Fleckner was right in that particular.

"We can give warning anonymously, however, through the telephonoscope," he insisted. "It's our duty to do so. Otherwise we become accessories to the crime."

There was a stubborn light in his eye. It was evident that the breach between the two men was widening rapidly. Though I sympathized with Priestley, I decided that it was unwise to take sides openly at present.

Fleckner started to speak, then hesitated and studied the other's face thoughtfully. Apparently he recalled previous experiences with his explosively idealistic associate and decided to temporize.

"Well, we'll watch the situation a little, and if there seems to be no chance by morning of the trust picking up the treasure again, we'll try to think up a method of carrying out your idea. Meantime there's no use of all of us staying awake. This is my watch. You boys both get some sleep. I'll call you, Priestley, at five, and Blair can relieve you at seven."

We agreed to that arrangement, and Priestley and I retired to sleeping-rooms off the laboratory and lay down half undressed.

I dozed fitfully at first, but presently found myself lying awake, puzzling over Miss Stimson's strange attack of nerves, wondering if it could possibly be that she was up to anything treacherous. Suddenly a concrete suggestion occurred to me. Could it be possible that she had frightened off Chandler purposely with the intention of making away with the treasure herself with the aid of confederates? Why not?

Full of new apprehension, I jumped out of bed, and throwing on a bathrobe, went out into the laboratory.

Professor Fleckner sat in his chair by the control board, where we had left him. But fatigue and monotony had proven too much for him. His chin rested on his chest. He was sound asleep.

I glanced nervously at the screen. One-half of it still revealed Chandler pacing the floor of his bedchamber as before. On the other half was the same stretch of lonely mountain forest road. I knew it positively by the big boulder with a scrub oak growing out of its base beside which the van had halted. But there was a difference. I rubbed my eyes and looked again. Then I seized the control lever and shifted it up and down the road and through the forest for miles each way. In vain.

The van and its two million dollar treasure had vanished utterly.

CHAPTER XII
The Crime Trust Retaliates

I NUDGED Fleckner's shoulder sharply. He awoke with a start.

"Humph! Been asleep!" he

ejaculated.

He glanced at the clock.

"Four o'clock! Dozed pretty nearly a half-hour! Three thirty when I looked last. How long you been out here? Anything happened?"

He looked at Chandler's restless image first, then at the section of mountain road. He, too, rubbed his eyes and looked again. Then he leaped to his feet excitedly.

"Where's the van?" he demanded. "You and Priestley been up to something?"

He whirled on me accusingly.

"Priestley is presumably still asleep," I replied coldly. "I just came out of my room. At any rate we could hardly have engineered the stealing in the few minutes you've been asleep, even if we could have done it without waking you."

But he seemed still suspicious of us. He tiptoed over to Priestley's room and looked in. I followed. I confess I wondered a little, preposterous as the idea seemed, if Priestley could have had a hand in it. But Priestley was sleeping the sound sleep of healthy exhaustion. Fleckner shook him roughly, and when he was awake told him what had happened. But he did not repeat the imputation he had hurled at me in the first excitement of his discovery. Priestley's astonishment seemed too genuine to be simulated.

Priestley came out, and under Fleckner's directions we each took a ray and made a systematic search of the hills all about the spot where the van had stood. The ground was frozen, and there was no snow, so we had no tracks to guide us.

At daybreak we gave it up and sat in discouraged discussion of many possible theories. My suspicions of the girl I kept to myself without knowing exactly why. Perhaps it was my consciousness of their vagueness. Possibly it was natural chivalry. It may have been the lingering appeal of a pair of violet eyes. I suspect it was all three. At any rate I contributed no suggestions of value, and neither of the other two thought of iss Stimson in connection with the vanished van.

Fleckner was inclined to fancy some belated motorist had discovered the van and salvaged it. In that case, if the finder was honest, he would advertise his find. It would make a most sensational news story, the finding of two million dollars out on a lonely road without a guardian. It would become even more sensational when it developed that no one had missed this tidy little sum, and that there were no lawful claimants for it.

Of course if the owner were dishonest he would hide his treasure-trove, and in the course of time try to use it. In that case he would doubtless give himself away eventually.

Priestley, however, stubbornly clung to the belief that Chandler had somehow got word to a confederate while Fleckner slept. That man, he believed, had flown out in a swift plane and taken the van to a safe hiding-place where it would await another attempt by the chief.

"That we'll be able to determine as soon as Chandler gets back in touch with his men," the professor decided.

At eight o'clock Miss Stimson returned to her duties as usual. There was no hint in her manner of any remaining embarrassment over the occurrences of the night before. Her green shade was in place again, so I caught no more glimpses of her disturbing eyes. Fleckner greeted her rather curtly, and Priestley with a politely impersonal inquiry as to her health.

But we were immediately afterward engrossed with Chandler's movements. He went back to town on the 8.30 train, and at 9.30 was closeted alone in his office in his town house. Immediately he went into the telephone booth and turned one of the secret rings. Fleckner swung on the direction-finder, and a moment later switched one telephonoscope ray on the little private dining-room where the telephone bell was ringing merrily.

Chandler, meantime, having started the call to the Riccadona, came out of the booth and began pacing the floor.

A few minutes later a waiter at the café, passing down the corridor, heard the bell in the private room. He went in and pressed a button at the side of the instrument and the ringing ceased. At the same instant the phone in Chandler's office gave one sharp ring, evidently a signal

that his call had been noted.

The waiter at the café hurried downstairs and to the desk.

"The other bell is ringing in No. 9," he said, and departed on his duties.

The cashier went into the phone booth back of him and called up Judge Tanner at his chambers.

"This is Tom," he said. "Your reservation for No. 9 is O. K."

Judge Tanner hung up the phone, put on his hat, and fifteen minutes later was in No. 9 at the Riccadona.

"An ingenious system for getting in touch with his gang at almost any time," Fleckner commented. "He didn't dare use it when he got in last night, I suppose, for fear a too unseasonable hour would arouse suspicion."

Tanner went through the form of ordering a breakfast, and then connected with Chandler's study by the wall phone. Chandler looked his intense relief when he found himself again in touch with his chief aid.

"The goods arrived at No. 20 on time, and the man in charge left after getting the signal, as agreed," Chandler related. "But the man sent to get them was trapped, and had to clear out and leave them.

"Some one jumped out of the bush and another voice, sounded like a woman's, he said, called for him to stop. He barely escaped. I don't think he was identified, but I didn't dare order a move for fear we'd been betrayed and would be caught. Send a discreet tracer over the road to see if he can locate the goods. Don't have him make a move to claim them unless it's perfectly safe. There may be a trap there. Set another tracer after the traitor."

Chandler hung up. The professor looked at Priestley triumphantly.

"What did I tell you?" he remarked tauntingly. "You see Chandler is as much in the dark as we are. I wonder, now, what could have happened to that van."

He looked speculatively through the open door to where Miss Stimson sat bent over her notes. I was afraid for a moment that he might be about to question her, but Judge Tanner claimed his attention.

The judge had connected with the underground clubroom and repeated Chandler's news to one of the black-robed brethren who immediately busied himself with a series of cryptic calls. As a result a swift airplane left an up-town hangar an hour later, its passenger an innocent-looking traveling salesman for the New York Sun Motor Company. He flew over Putnam County back and forth for hours at a three-mile level, his plane blurred by a thin screen of vapor, scouring the earth with a powerful fieldglass.

At the same time the New York State Agency for the Heatless Light Company decided suddenly to put its field force on for an intensive house to house campaign in Putnam County. Every canvasser, our records showed, was a member of the crime trust.

Also, during the day, word was sent in cipher to every district representative in the country, and the dragnet was thoroughly set for the missing van.

Meanwhile we, as well as the agents for the trust, were scouring every edition of the papers for a story of the finding of a mysterious van loaded with treasure. But the day passed without news, and the day lengthened into a fruitless week. The judge took all his meals at the Riccadona, and had long conferences with Chandler, which brought them nowhere.

During all this time the trust company continued doing business without the slightest suspicion of its loss.

At length, on the eighth night after the disappearance of the van, Tanner got a call from a man in the secret clubroom who was a new one to us. Apparently, from the conversation that followed, he was in charge of a section appointed to ferret out and punish traitors. In the confusion of trying to watch all the complicated communications sent out the day after the robbery, we had evidently overlooked this particular thread in the tangled skein.

"We think we've located a traitor," this man declared. "We haven't positive evidence, but it's pretty strong. We believe he knows nothing of what became of the van later, but probably he had a grievance and tipped off the State police, who nearly caught the man sent to meet the van. We believe the police are keeping the facts from the public, hoping to trap us."

"I'll call you back in a few minutes," said the judge.

Then he switched to Chandler and reported.

"What do you recommend?" Chandler asked.

"We'd better take no chances," the judge advised. "Suppose we're mistaken. Better to sacrifice an innocent man than run the slightest risk of having the lot of us caught."

"You're right," Chandler agreed. "Use your judgment."

Tanner switched back to the detective.

"The order is to take extreme measures," he reported.

The detective left the phone booth and strolled about the main room. After a moment he jogged an elbow of a man he passed, and a few minutes latter met him in one of the little council-rooms.

"No. 72 is condemned," the detective said laconically.

"I'll attend to him at once," the other responded in a most matter-of-fact tone. "Any idea who he is?"

"Not the slightest," replied the other. "That's for you to find out."

"I'll shoot a little perfume into his clothes, and identify him outside."

"Very good!" agreed the other. We all sat chilled with horror as the sense of impending tragedy dawned on us.

Priestley was the first to speak.

"This is murder!" he gasped. "We must stop it."

"We'll have no exposures at present," Fleckner declared sternly. "We've mixed things up enough already."

Priestley remained silent, but I knew he was unconvinced.

The executioner roamed about the main room until he came upon No. 72 standing in a little group about a billiard-table watching a game. The executioner had taken from his pocket a small atomizer filled with a colorless fluid. Holding this in his hand under his robe he casually walked up behind his victim, and pretending to become absorbed in the game, placed the nozzle of the atomizer against the other's back and pressed the bulb.

"Carrying odors is the one thing the telephonoscope won't do." Fleckner remarked.

The scent must have been a delicate one, for no one about the billiard-table gave any signs of noting an offensive odor. The executioner strolled away after a moment and a little later signaled another man to one side.

"I've put the scent on a victim," he whispered. "Go up and stand at the store end of the exit. Trail any one who comes out that way with the scent on his clothes. I'll take the other exit."

The executioner then left the club, appearing presently in ordinary clothes on the sidewalk in front of the rear entrance to the little tobacco shop. He was a dapper-looking, blond young man, having the appearance of a gilded youth with nothing on his mind. Presently his assistant, a pale dark fellow, rather slouchily dressed, took up his post in the store.

It was over an hour before No. 72 emerged. He went directly to the street, almost brushing against the dapper little man who had been ordered to kill him.

The executioner gave no sign of noticing the heavy, uninteresting-looking stranger who walked by him and down into the street, but we noted that his nostrils dilated and his eyes gleamed with satisfaction. He crossed the avenue leisurely, and keeping his prey in sight, strolled along in the direction he was following.

"Do you mean to say you refuse to prevent a murder?" Priestley demanded, fiercely turning on Fleckner.

The professor winced a little, but held his ground.

"I absolutely refuse," he said. "There is nothing we could do that wouldn't give us away now and spoil our future plans. It's too risky. Anyhow, the fellow deserves death."

Priestley stood over him with clenched fists, his face a blaze of fury.

"I warned you once before," Fleckner interposed hastily, "that if you resist me it will be disastrous to your fortune and your reputation, as well as to the good you hope to accomplish in the world by your investment."

I fully expected to see Priestley defy him at any cost. Instead, after a moment, he pulled himself together and turned on his heel.

"Very well," he muttered. "At any rate I won't stay and see murder committed. I'm going out for a while till it's over."

"Good!" Fleckner exclaimed in relief. "You've stuck too close here. Your nerves are unstrung. Better run home and get some sleep. I'll call you if anything interesting happens."

Priestley went out without another word.

I had a fleeting thought that we ought to keep Priestley covered by one of our rays, but checked the idea without voicing it. Such a suggestion to Fleckner might seem to indicate suspicion of my new friend. Anyhow, the professor and I had about all we could attend to alone. Miss Stimson was in the other room catching up on some neglected records, which left only two of us to keep the ramifications of the trust plot on the screen at once.

I wished many times afterward that I had obeyed my impulse to trail Priestley.

Meantime the victim of the trust's suspicion continued on to his home a few blocks down, went in, and after a little, to bed. His shadower, after carefully studying the surroundings from the outside, entered the apartment-house where his victim had just disappeared and said to the hall attendant:

"I came to call on some one who I think just came in—the thick-set dark gentleman."

"You mean Mr. Gersten?"

"Gersten? Doesn't seem as if that was his name. I met him only once and I've lost his card. I have a business appointment with him. What apartment is he in?"

"Sixtieth floor, apartment 21."

"Oh, that's not he, then. The man I'm after lives on the thirty-first floor. Isn't this apartment-house No. 1,239?"

"Oh, no. it's No. 1,241."

"Ah! I've mistaken the house." He went out hastily with the information he sought. Apparently the blow was not to fall at once, for he took the subway, and a little later reached his own home and went to bed.

But here again our vigilant rays missed something, as it turned out later.

Fleckner, seeing no likelihood of any more excitement that night, left one ray fixed on the sleeping form of Gersten, alias No. 72, another on the underground club, and a third on Gersten's would-be executioner. Chandler and Tanner of course also held a place on other sections, but they, too, were asleep.

Fleckner stretched himself wearily, looked at the clock, and called Miss Stimson.

There was no reply.

"She's gone some time ago," I remarked. "It's long past time."

"She should have spoken to me before she went," he said irritably.

At that moment a door slammed outside. There was a clatter of feet in the ante-room. The laboratory door burst open and Miss Stimson hurled herself in.

"They've got him! They've got him!" she cried.

We sprang to our feet in astonishment. "Got whom? What do you mean? Who are they?" demanded the professor.

"Mr. Priestley—he tried to save Mr. Gersten—the trust caught him and took him away in a cab—I tried to trail it—lost it!"

She sank to the floor in a faint.

CHAPTER XIII
At Grips With the Crime Trust

WE stared in doubt and amazement at the limp figure of the girl. Then by common impulse we searched the screen to verify her startling announcement of the kidnaping of Priestley. All was quiet around the apartment house in which Gersten, the condemned trust agent, lived. There was no sign of disturbance in the apartment itself. Gersten was still sleeping peacefully without any appearance of having moved since we last looked at his reflected image.

Fleckner began frantically trying out all the telephonoscope connections we had—the young assassin chief in his home, the underground club, even Chandler. No sign of activity. He even swept the ray up and down the quiet streets radiating from Gersten's home peering in every taxicab, hoping to find the one in which Priestley had been taken prisoner. But that was a futile proceeding begotten of panic and he quickly abandoned it.

Certain it was that Priestley had not arrived home. He made doubly certain of that by searching the house and calling the drowsy butler on the telephone.

Meantime. I was doing what I could to restore the girl to her senses. She revived presently, but it was some time before she could tell a coherent story. Even then she was strangely reticent and evasive at some points in her narrative.

"I heard Mr. Priestley arguing with Professor Fleckner about trying to keep the trust from murdering this man Gersten," she said. "When Mr. Priestley went by my desk something in the way he looked and walked made me think he was going to try to interfere with those murderers all by himself. I knew he would be in great danger. I thought I might help him or at least warn the police if necessary.

"I followed without his knowing it. I don't believe he knows me anyhow with my hat and coat on and my eye-shade off. He went to the public phone booths on the corner and called up Mr. Gersten. I listened in. I can't tell you how I managed it. I learned the secret when I was a telephone manager before I came here. Do you know that Mr. Gersten, this No. 72 we've been watching, is an old friend of Mr. Priestley?

" 'Hello, John, this is Tom Priestley,' he said when he got his connection.

" 'Why, hello, Tom,' Gersten answered, 'where you been keeping yourself and what do you mean pulling a man out of bed this time of night?'

" 'Listen, John,' he said, 'your life's in danger. I've just overheard a gang you've got mixed up with plotting to kill you. They think you've been betraying them. They're watching your place now. I can't tell you any more. You'll know best how to handle it. I advise you to call up the district attorney himself in the morning and get protection. Stay off the street. You'll know how to handle it better than I, anyhow. You know the gang. I'll help you if I can. I think I know a way. I can't tell you more. I'm surprised to find you're in with such a gang, but I can't see you killed!' "

"But," Fleckner broke in, "Gersten didn't talk with any one on the phone. We've been watching him right along. He's been asleep."

"Then it's just as I thought." the girl exclaimed. "One of the trust tapped his phone circuit with an instrument as soon as they located him at home. He disguised his voice and answered instead of Gersten when Mr. Priestley called. That's how they trapped him.

"Mr. Priestley came out of the telephone station and started to walk back here. I watched him from across the street. A man hurried along by him in the same direction and must have sprayed an anesthetic in his face, because Mr.

Priestley stopped suddenly and staggered. The strange man turned and caught him before he fell. Just then a cab whirled up. A man stepped out and helped the other man put Mr. Priestley in the cab. Then they both got in and drove away. I started to scream, but saw a policeman coming and knew I mustn't attract the police. They'd kill Mr. Priestley right away if they thought the police were after them. As it is they'll keep him alive for a while and try to discover what he knows. I couldn't find a cab to follow in so I came back here. That's all, but you must find him quick. You must!"

She showed signs of becoming hysterical. We tried to question her, but all she would say was—

"Get your rays to work. Don't bother with me! I don't know any more."

There seemed to be nothing to do but follow her advice. But though we searched for the rest of the night we accomplished nothing more than to verify Miss Stimson's belief that the trust agents had killed the telephone antenna connecting with the instrument in Gersten's apartment by the use of a high power wave sender which burned out the delicate connections. They had then evidently tuned their own outlaw instrument into the same wave length and, as she had surmised, answered his calls. We tried the expedient of calling up his number, but apparently the listeners-in now suspected a trap and re-fused to answer.

At half-past eight in the morning our screen showed Judge Tanner appearing for breakfast in the private dining-room at the Riccadona. Immediately he called the underground club and got a report from the assassin chief.

"I identified No. 72 and had him trailed. He'll die a natural death within twenty-four hours if you say the word. But something happened again. Things are going wrong and it's getting on my nerves. I'm even beginning to wonder if 72 is guilty. Anyhow he isn't the only one. You know young Tom Priestley, the Priestley millionaire? Well, it seems he's a friend of 72 and tried to call him up late last night and warn him. We cut in and caught Priestley and are holding him for orders.

"The question now is, is Priestley a member of the organization? If he is he's a traitor. If he isn't then there's a leak to the outside and we've got to find it and see how far it's gone and kill as many people as is necessary to stop it or our whole game is up."

Judge Tanner turned pale and trembled visibly as he got this startling information. He thought for some moments before replying.

"I'll call you back," he managed to say at last.

He cut off the assassin chief and rang on Chandler. In a halting manner strangely at variance with the suave judge's usually assured address, he broke the news to his unknown chief who was hardly less affected by it than his subordinate.

"This connects up with the disappearance of the van-load of money, Chandler ruminated. "It's a deeper plot than we thought. Tell your men to keep this Priestley alive till they've got all they can out of him. Find out, if possible, if he belongs to the organization. Try the supreme sign on him. No use to try tracing back through the recruiting chain. Every one is bound to name no names unless of a proven traitor. They'd suspect trickery and refuse for the most part. Get at it quick. Meantime let 72 live till this is cleared up."

Tanner transmitted these orders back to the assassin, who promptly left the clubroom. We followed this fellow closely all day with our ray, but learned nothing of Priestley's whereabouts. He talked with numerous people and telephoned frequently, but apparently when treachery was afoot all members of the trust used excessive precautions. All communications were strictly in a code and quite different from the one he had previously unraveled.

By evening we were in the depths of despair and alarm. Professor Fleckner and I managed to preserve a moderately calm exterior, but Miss Stimson was frankly hysterical over the situation. We sat in the laboratory by the telephonoscope screen all that night, dozing at intervals from sheer weariness but for the most part trying many new but futile angles of ray-search

and debating various schemes of learning Priestley's whereabouts and effecting a rescue.

I was all for trying a scheme of scaring some one of the members higher up in the trust into revealing Priestley's hiding-place, by using our ray projector and presenting one of our images, carefully disguised, to the right man.

"But," Fleckner objected. "whom would you approach? Chandler? Tanner? Any of the others whom we have identified positively as concerned in Priestley's disappearance? I doubt if any one of them, even the chief assassin, knows where he is. That detail has been left to agents whom we haven't placed yet. If any one, excepting Chandler himself, was frightened into trying to find Priestley, they'd simply kill him and Priestley's jailer. Then maybe your suggestion might work. Failing that, I'll try the lever on Chandler. I'm not hopeful of the result. Conditions aren't ripe yet for a direct approach to that gentleman, but we can't afford to risk leaving Priestley with them until he breaks down and gives us all away."

I had a feeling as he spoke that the old man was more concerned for his own safety and the success of his schemes than he was for Priestley himself. Nevertheless his argument appealed to me as sound.

It was nearly eight in the morning when I awoke with a start, after a longer doze than usual. Miss Stimson had arisen and crossed over to where Professor Fleckner sat moodily studying the screen. Her hysteria had passed. There was in its place an air of calm determination.

"Professor Fleckner," she announced coolly, "I'll release Mr. Priestley."

"You!" he shouted in amazement.

"How?" I demanded.

"I can't tell you how, not at present anyhow. Just let me go for a while. Meantime keep Mr. Chandler covered closely. You remember he is to be out at conferences all day today."

She went out before we recovered sufficiently from our amazement to make any comment.

"What do you make of it?" Fleckner demanded. "Is the girl crazy? She's certainly acted strangely ever since that night when she warned Chandler away from that van-load of money."

"I don't know," I admitted. "I do think she admires our friend Priestley greatly and his danger may have unbalanced her a little. I think it would be wise to keep one of the rays on her while she is out. If she goes wild altogether we can warn a policeman to take her in charge and pay no attention to what she says."

"Good idea," he agreed.

He got Miss Stimson on the screen before she reached the street. We watched her progress from then on with such absorbing interest that it became almost impossible to keep our other rays ad-justed properly on all the persons we were trying to watch at once.

The girl went first to her home in an apartment a few blocks away and when she came out again she was veiled and dressed so differently that it was hard to recognize in her, the demure little office mouse of the green eyeshade. She went by subway up to the street corner nearest to Chandler's home. There she ascended to the upper street level and a position in a public telephone station opposite the Chandler home where she could watch it through an open window.

In a little while the President-elect came out, got into his car and was driven away. We had half expected the girl to waylay and plead with him or make some wild threat. Fleckner was on the point of projecting my image before a police officer on the next corner and having the girl apprehended before she took any such disastrous step. But to our relief Chandler was driven off without any move on her part.

Instead we were amazed to see her calmly cross the street and push the announcer button at the Chandler front door.

"I wish to see Mrs. Simmons. the housekeeper," she announced with quiet dignity when the butler appeared. "I am a friend of hers."

A few minutes later a gray haired woman of about sixty appeared and regarded her caller with considerable perplexity.

They were in a small reception room off the main hall. The girl stepped past the housekeeper and to that good woman's obvious amazement, softly closed the door.

Then she turned back to the housekeeper and before the latter could protest, she raised a warning hand.

"Don't give me away, Mrs. Simmons. Some one might overhear."

With that she raised her veil.

The woman choked back an exclamation. Her face showed mingled affection and alarm.

"You? Here?" she whispered.

"I had to look inside once more. I watch for him sometimes. I saw him drive away just now. I couldn't resist one more peep. Can't you take me up to his study where he lives so much? If any of the family see me, say it's a young friend of yours you're taking up to your rooms and wanted to show around a little."

The girl's voice trembled and there were tears in her eyes. If she was acting, it was an exceedingly clever bit of work.

Fleckner chuckled dryly.

"Another dark chapter in the good Chandler's life. I certainly am surprised at Miss Stimson, however."

The housekeeper hesitated.

"It's a risk," she said, "but you know I'd do anything for you, Ruth."

The good woman was weeping quietly.

"That's the same dear old Mrs. Simmons!" the girl exclaimed, patting her on the shoulder.

Mrs. Simmons opened the door and peered out. There was no one in the hall. She motioned the girl to follow and they went cautiously out and up a rear elevator that led directly into Chandler's study on the top floor.

The girl sank in a chair and gazed raptly about her for some minutes. Finally she roused herself with an effort and glanced at her watch.

"Oh, I promised to phone a friend at ten!" she exclaimed. "May I use this one?"

She indicated the booth containing the phone with the secret attachments through which we had so often watched Chandler issue orders to his followers.

"Why certainly, dearie," the housekeeper agreed.

Miss Stimson entered the booth, closed the sound-proof door and then, to our sudden illumination, twisted the ring that threw on the secret connection with the little dining-room at the Riccadona where Judge Tanner was just finishing his breakfast.

A moment later she was giving orders to the deluded agent of the crime trust in the same husky half-whisper in which the real head of that disreputable band was wont to issue his mandates.

CHAPTER XIV
Miss Stimson Uses Direct Methods

THE sheer audacity of the girl took our breath away. What her former connection with the Chandler household had been I could not imagine, for the sinister suggestion made by Fleckner somehow did not ring true. My instincts rebelled against it. Then there was the evident respect of that manifestly conventional Mrs. Simmons.

But another possibility flashed into my mind. Had this girl all along been an agent of the crime trust spying upon us? Would that account for the episode of the treasure van? If so why had she not betrayed us long before? On the other hand she was now evidently working against the organization. Had her devotion to Priestley, which I had been quietly noting, converted her to our side? I wondered if Professor Fleckner had thought of these startling possibilities and what action he might take.

But be all that as it might, her quick feminine mind had grasped a simple and direct plan of action and she had the courage to carry it out promptly. We gasped in admiration at her boldness and ingenuity as we listened to the orders she was giving to Judge Tanner over the secret telephone.

"I've just got some important information about our latest prisoner, young Priestley," she whispered, and from Judge Tanner's expression it was evident that he was entirely deceived by the disguised voice. "He is refusing to give infor-mation about the rest of his crowd because he expects to be rescued soon. They had advance information somehow as to where he was to be hidden and they have a number of our men spotted. We've got to make a quick shift and get him in the hands of an entirely new group that they're not yet wise to. My plan is to let him escape and pull the old crowd off his trail altogether. Then while he's free he'll go straight to his men. My new bunch of trailers will follow and we'll grab the whole gang. What do you think of that scheme?"

"An excellent one!" Tanner agreed, enthusiastically.

"That girl has a great head!" Fleckner exclaimed. "I never half appreciated her before. But I don't quite understand it. I don't think I can ever trust her again. She's too clever and women arc flighty, vari-able creatures at best. And there's been some sort of tie between her and Chandler. That's evident."

Fleckner was too absorbed in present happenings to follow out his reasoning but for me a sudden light was shed on her hysterical performance which had frightened Chandler away from the treasure van that night just as he was about to lead us to the main treasure. The girl, I was convinced, had acted with a purpose on that occasion. She had not wanted Chandler to guide us to the Treasures of Tanta-lus. Was it sentiment for Chandler that prompted her or had she an in-terest in the treasure itself? That was what bothered me. At any rate, she seemed now to be acting in our behalf.

But was she? That was another question that popped into my head a second later. Priestley, released from the trust, would be in her power. Was he safe there? Or was the girl a deserter from the trust and was now a member of a rival gang which, through her aid, had stolen the treasure van and was now cleverly using Professor Fleckner's great invention for its own ends?

That last fleeting suspicion seemed at that moment so fantastic that I instantly dismissed it and gave my undivided attention to the screen again.

"This is my plan," the girl was saying. "Follow closely and act quickly. There's no time to lose. Get your present attendants on Priestley out of the way as far and fast and secretly as you can. Look out for trailers. Have a new man bring him in a cab down to the Esplanade in Van Cortlandt Park, arriving there exactly at noon. My new men will be on hand to trail him to his gang. Right at the center of the Esplanade in front of the Wright statue have him slow down and tell Priestley that he had been ordered to take him away and kill him, but that he couldn't commit murder, so he was going to rebel and let him escape. Then have him untie Priestley and turn him loose. Have the man drive away as quickly as possible. My other men will do the rest."

Tanner agreed without comment as was his custom on getting commands from Chandler. His careful repetition of the orders to his agent in the underground club made it evident that he suspected nothing wrong.

But again from there on we lost the trail in the confusion of multiple messages all in code. This time, however, it was not important that we should trace the orders further.

For promptly at noon, we enjoyed the immense relief of seeing Miss Stimson's directions carried out to the letter.

Van Cortlandt Park Esplanade, even in those days, was thronged with noon-hour strollers from the factories along its southern margin, and a steady stream of motors filled its roadways. Miss Stimson could not have chosen a better place in which to carry out her scheme than this spot where any slightly unusual occurrence would pass unnoticed in the throng. For a half hour before the appointed time we swept the locality with our ray, studying every loiterer to see if we recognized a known trust agent, but we failed to see any familiar face or suspicious character.

It was exactly twelve o'clock when a cab, which had been circling slowly around the Esplanade, drew up and stopped for a moment in front of the Wright statue.

The door opened and Priestley stepped out, a pale and haggard Priestley, but with bearing undaunted. He stood for a moment in front of the statue and looked about him suspiciously. The cab drove rapidly away.

Just then he noticed Miss Stimson strolling toward the statue. She was dressed differently than in the morning, but was still veiled. Catching sight of Priestley, she stepped up to him briskly.

"Good morning," she greeted him cheerily. "You are a little late." Then she added quickly in an undertone, "It's Miss Stimson. Don't look surprised. You're safe now but we can't be too careful."

Priestley rose to the occasion and checked his momentary confusion with a laugh.

"I didn't see you coming and you startled me," he said. "I'm sorry I'm late. What can I do to atone?"

"You can buy me a nice luncheon at Briarcliff Inn. My car is right over here. I'm going to show you how fast a real lady can drive."

This debonair, easy-speaking young woman was still another Miss Stimson to us. I realized more than ever that the girl was a consummate actress.

She led the way across to the parking station and they entered a swift-looking little coupé. The girl backed the car skilfully out of the line and it glided swiftly away northward.

Then, just as we swung the ray forward to follow the speeding coupé a cab flashed on the other side of the screen breaking all speed limits in defiance of the traf-

fic officer at the southern entrance of the Esplanade.

"Better throw on another ray and investigate that cab," Professor Fleckner directed anxiously as he adjusted the ray he was controlling, so that we might keep a close-up of Miss Stimson's coupé on the screen.

I swung in a second ray and as I picked up the interior of the cab, my instinctive fear was realized. It was the cab which had brought Priestley to the Wright statue just now, still driven by the man who had released him. This man's face was a picture of desperate fear. Beside him sat another man, registering both anger and alarm in his pugnacious countenance. They were both straining their eyes toward Miss Stimson's fleeing car into which they had evidently seen Priestley enter.

The situation was as evident as though it had been told in words. Miss Stimson's haste had been justified. Somewhere along the line the crime trust's momentarily deluded gang had discovered the trick played on them. The second man in the pursuing cab had evidently been sent in haste to undo the error and arrived near the scene in time to meet the man who had just released Priestley.

And for the moment it seemed that Miss Stimson's clever artifice had been wasted. All unconscious of pursuit, she was driving northward as fast as speed regulations permitted, but far too slowly to keep ahead of the pursuing cab for more than a few minutes.

The crime trust's agent, in his desperation, hurled speed regulations to the winds. Pedestrians fled in every direction. Vehicles shot toward the curbing to the right and left.

"Warn the girl! I'll get a traffic officer after the cab!" I shouted to Fleckner above the tumult of the crowd and the snorting of motor-horns that filled our little room from our sounding screen as though we were actually on the edge of the throng.

Fleckner projected his voice into the coupé, warned the girl with a word, and in terror she threw her car into full speed and shot out of the Esplanade into a park road, with the swiftness of an airplane. At that she was barely holding her own against the swiftly pursuing cab.

In less than a minute, some quarter of a mile away, I located a motor-cycle traffic-officer, trundling his machine leisurely along, the speeders hidden from his sight by a clump of shrubbery.

To avoid creating public consternation by a seeming- miracle I projected my image among the bushes and seemed to step out of them into the path of the officer.

"There's a speeder playing havoc with the crowd over there!" I shouted excitedly, pointing across the Esplanade.

Without a question he jumped on his cycle and was gone like a flash. Hopefully I drew my image back into the bushes and cut off the projector. If the officer should overhaul and arrest the driver of the cab, it would give our friends a chance after all.

Breathlessly Fleckner and I followed the triple race on our screen; the coupé slowly losing its lead over the recklessly driven cab, but—thank Heaven!—the motor-cycle gaining on it much more rapidly.

They left Van Cortlandt Park behind and flew up the Yonkers Boulevard. A few minutes later they were swinging perilously around the sharp curves of the Westchester Park drives.

Meantime Miss Stimson, behind the screen of her car top, had been ordering a lightning change act that seemed rather futile under the circumstances. Under her directions Priestley had hauled a feminine outfit—cape, skirt, hat, veil and gloves—from under the seat and put them on over his own clothing. Without too close inspection he looked like a large-framed middle-aged woman.

Miss Stimson turned the wheel over to him while she changed her own hat, veil and jacket for an assortment of entirely different style. She looked fifteen years older and a dowdy contrast to the trim, stylish figure of a few minutes before.

She evidently hoped to get out of sight of her pursuers long enough to turn about and, in these disguises, give them the slip. Fleckner heartened her by telling her that the motor officer might give her that chance, though a dubious one at best.

Within five minutes that hope seemed about to be realized. The motor-cycle drew along side the cab and its rider signaled the driver to stop. Then our hopes were dashed again.

The second man in the cab turned back his coat lapel and, to our consternation, displayed the badge of a Central Office detective. He shouted something to the motor-cycle officer and the latter, instead of insisting on stopping the cab, let his cycle's speed out another notch and shot by in pursuit of the coupé.

By invoking the aid of the law we had merely made the capture of our friends doubly sure. The trust had played the same game. It was only a matter of minutes now when the motor-cycle would overtake them and Miss Stimson's pitiful little subterfuge would avail them nothing. The pursuers had long since noted the number and style of the car.

But just as I was in despair, the genius of Fleckner again came to the rescue.

"Let me handle your lever a minute, Blair," he exclaimed suddenly. "Get one of those spare lengths of power cable out of the storeroom."

"Now," he directed, when I had brought the small roll containing about a rod of half-inch wire cable, "bend one end so it will hook over that window-catch, then carry the other end across the room stretch-ing it in front of the screen. I'll turn on the magnifier and then project this cable so it appears in image like a two-inch hawser stretched across the road in front of that mo-tor-cycle and cab. That'll stop 'em for a minute, I'll guarantee."

The scheme worked. The motor-cycle and the cab flew around the bend and their drivers saw across the road a few rods ahead, what ap-peared to be a heavy cable stretched taut at a height that meant a sure wrecking for both vehicles. Brakes screeched and they came to a dead stop within two yards of the appar-ent obstruction.

All three men swore roundly and stared stupidly at the cable. The speeding coupé in the meantime lengthened its lead by a quarter of a mile.

"They've stopped," Fleckner told Miss Stimson, again projecting his voice into the coupé. "Better slip off on a by-path and trust to throwing them off the scent. They'll be on again in a moment."

"I'll do better than that," replied the girl calmly. She brought the car to a grinding halt, reversed and turned squarely around. She threw over the lever beside the seat and the coupé top folded down out of sight leaving the car looking like an ordinary open roadster. Thereupon she pulled out false number plates from under the seat, hooked them over the old ones and was back in the car in barely a minute.

At the same instant the motor-cycle officer, who by good chance had not yet attempted to touch the unsubstantial cable image, started to shove his machine under the obstruction to go on with the pursuit.

"Snatch it loose and pretend to run," Fleckner directed me.

I jerked the end of the cable off the window-catch and went through a pantomime of running. Professor Fleckner threw my projected image across the park green apparently dragging the cable after me.

"I'll get him! You two go on," shouted the pseudo detective leaping from the cab.

He raced after my image pouring a stream of automatic pistol bullets at it till Fleckner ran it into a thicket and dissolved the thing. How long my supposed pursuer beat about that bush in search of a mirage I don't know, for I had more important matters on hand.

The fellow was barely out of the cab, when it leaped into full speed with the motor-cycle already gaining on it in an effort to make up for lost time.

And around the next bend they barely avoided collision with an open roadster containing apparently a pair of middle-aged ladies to whom they accorded hardly a glance as they swept by.

CHAPTER XV
A Chamber of Horrors

AN hour later, to our immense relief, we welcomed Miss Stimson and Priestley, still in their outlandish disguises,

back into the safe shelter of the laboratory. Immediately after meeting their deluded pursuers, they had turned off the road over which they had been fleeing and worked south over a circuitous route until they reached the Getty Square garage where Miss Stimson had rented the car, a new interchangeable model that had admirably suited her purposes. The false number-plates she had made herself with card-board and a little paint.

In returning the car, disguised as she was, she avoided the garageman's suspicion by saying that she was bringing it back for her sister who had rented it.

In the meantime, as our following ray showed, the motor-cycle officer and the man in the cab ran on for over a mile before they became convinced that they had lost the scent. Then they turned back looking for clues, but of course, in vain. Finally they came to the point where they had dropped the supposed Central Office man. There the motorcycle officer left them and so did we, for we saw no profit in following them further.

Priestley was too worn and exhausted with his experience to talk at first. Fleckner's man brought him some food which he ate in silence. Then he retired to the room he had been using and slept for twelve hours straight.

Meantime Fleckner, Miss Stimson and I took turns at watching the screens and resting, but whatever action the chief men of the crime trust had taken on Priestley's escape had been put through while we were distracted by the chase. We never did learn how Chandler found out so soon the trick that had been played on him. By the time we got him and Tanner and the others back on the screen, whatever excitement it had caused had subsided or been suppressed.

Nevertheless, we soon learned that appropriate action had been started.

When Priestley finally awoke, about six the next morning, I had also just finished my last nap of the night. He followed me out into the laboratory where Fleckner sat in front of the screen, which at this hour in the morning showed nothing but a series of pictures of still life—a choice assortment of sleeping villains.

"Where is Miss Stimson? I want to thank her properly for rescuing me. I was too groggy last night," were almost his first words.

"I sent Miss Stimson home about an hour ago," said Fleckner. "She insisted on watching with us on and off all night and she was pretty well worn out to begin with. Too excited to sleep, I guess. I made her go home where she could get away from the atmosphere for a while."

"She's a remarkable young woman," Priestley declared. "Do you know, I've paid so little attention to her that at this moment I hardly know what her face looks like. She wears that confounded eye shade all the time around here and

has a veil on whenever she goes out."

"She's a good deal of a mystery," Fleckner admitted. "I don't suppose she explained to you what connection she had with the Chandler household in the past?"

"No, she told me only the barest details of how she fooled Judge Tanner. She said she knew Chandler's housekeeper when she was a little girl and that helped her in getting in. What do you mean?"

Fleckner related in detail what took place in Chandler's house when Miss Stimson entered it the morning before.

"Strange, isn't it?" was Priestley's only comment, but I saw he was deeply disturbed and that he resented Fleckner's innuendoes.

"But come!" the professor demanded impatiently. "What about you? You have the story we're most anxious to hear. What happened when they grabbed you?"

Priestley shuddered. It was some minutes before he answered. When he did it was slowly, falteringly as a sufferer speaks between spasms of pain.

"It's an experience hard to talk about!" he said at last. "What I have to tell won't help us much. It's merely an exposition of what the crime trust will do to a man when it gets him in its clutches."

He paused for a moment and then with visible effort continued:

"During all the time I was in their hands I saw no one, and talked to no one directly, except the man who let me go. I saw him for a moment or two only just before he left me and he was evidently so disguised that I wouldn't recognize him again. They're exceedingly clever in their disguises. I'm convinced that when they have to work together in the open, as when they robbed the trust company, they are disguised even from each other. I haven't the slightest idea where they kept me or how I got there and came away.

"To begin with, I believe Miss Stimson has already told you that No. 72, the man named Gersten, whom the trust condemned as a traitor is, or rather was, an old friend of mine. We were chums in college and for a time I was engaged to his sister, but we broke the engagement by mutual agreement and later she married Paul Tilford, another close friend of mine. Gersten became an electrical engineer and has apparently been quite successful. His wife is an intimate friend of my sister. So you see how close is the tie between us and how great a shock it was when I found, not only that he was a criminal but that he was about to be murdered.

"It may be all right to view a prospective murder impersonally, especially when you feel that the world will be better off with the victim out of the way, but instincts revolted against allowing it to go on and as you remember, I protested. When I realized how helpless I was in the matter and how much

greater things were at stake, I gave in.

"But when I found the victim was to be John Gersten, I had to do something. To think that he is one of the criminal defectives! And the others we had discovered in the last few months! It is appalling! It makes one wonder whom he can trust; the whole world seems crime mad under its smug cover of conventional respectability. It makes one distrust his very self.

"At any rate I rushed out from here and did the utterly reckless thing of trying to call up and warn Gersten, you know.

"I came out of the phone booth and started down the street. I vaguely recall meeting a man, who passed me so closely that our elbows almost grazed. I was too preoccupied to notice him at all. And that instant I had a sudden dizzy feeling and then everything went black. That's all I know about my kidnaping. Of course, the man who passed me must have sprayed an anesthetic in my face.

"When I came to I was in total darkness and absolute silence. I might have been in an old-fashioned grave for all I could tell. In fact the close air added to that impression. I was lying on my back, on what seemed to be a slab of stone or concrete. I tried to move but found that my hands and feet were shackled.

"About my head was fastened some sort of contraption that seemed to consist mainly of pads over my ears and mouth, which I thought was to keep me from hearing sounds or calling for help, but I was quickly undeceived.

"Following the instinct to call for help, I tried to cry out and, to my surprise, succeeded amazingly. I emitted a thunderous sound, which seemed to be concentrated in my own ears. It nearly burst my ear drums.

"At that I heard a low chuckle. I stiffened and wrenched at my shackles, but was unable to break free.

" 'So you are awake, are you, Priestley?' some one said in a low casual tone, that came apparently from right beside me. I strained my eyes to see him but couldn't make out the slightest outline in the dense blackness.

" 'No use yelling your head off or straining yourself trying to break away,' the voice warned; 'that outfit on your head is a telephone receiver and transmitter so that you can hear what we have to say and tell us what we want to know. That's your only connection with the outside world, excepting a tube through which we'll feed you a little air if you want to use it to talk with and talk right.'

" 'Where am I?' I demanded.

"Again came the taunting chuckle, but somewhat louder.

" 'I can't give you the street and number, very well. It isn't allowed, but, if it'll be any consolation to you, I can tell you that you're in a strong aluminoid coffin buried under ten feet of earth in an unused subcellar. I'm the only one in the world who knows where you are, and I own the building, so you can see what a lively chance of rescue you have.'

"For once in my life I nearly fainted away with horror. I believed instinctively that he was telling the truth, though I never got further proof of it than his bare statement and my own impression of my surroundings.

" 'Now, whenever you are ready to tell us who are the rest of your friends who think they know some of our secrets, I will listen and if what you tell me is true, your situation will be made easier for you,' went on the voice.

"Just what I said in reply doesn't matter. I gave him to understand he had better kill me at once and save his time as I wasn't the kind of yellow dog who would find life tolerable after he had betrayed his friends. That wasn't, as a matter of fact, as heroic as it sounds, for I knew how badly they wanted to know the names of their enemies. They could gain nothing by killing me, for as long as they kept me a prisoner I could do them no harm. On the other hand if they did kill me, they'd lose their only present chance of learning the names of those who were endangering their whole organization. If I gave them the information, they'd have no further use for me and would doubtless promptly kill me. I knew they would try to keep me alive in the hope of finally breaking down my resistance. Every moment gained was giving you people so much more chance of rescuing me. I didn't realize the chances against the rescue or the torture I would go through meantime or I think I would have wished to die right then."

Priestley paused and shuddered again at the recollection of it.

"Did either of you ever happen to use that instrument of misery the old-fashioned wired telephone, whose connections were made by hand at switchboards—one of those complicated contrivances, generally out of order and at best working in most haphazard fashion, from which our fathers suffered a century ago? You may remember them as a boy, Professor Fleckner. Blair may have seen one in a museum. Well, when I was a youngster, about fifteen, I ran across a short line of that sort while traveling with my father in a back-woods section of northern Alaska. I remember well the mixture of buzz, clack and rattle that nearly split my ear-drums while the so-called 'Central' was trying, quite often in vain, to 'get a number,' with an especially violent attack preceding her frequent announcement that 'the line is busy.'

"Well, the telephone instrument that was attached to my head had the same set of tricks. Whether it was really an old-fashioned early-twentieth-century affair, I don't know. You have read of the ancient practise of torturing prisoners by a steady drip, drip of water on the shaven skull, or of the amiable art of tickling a victim to death, or driving him insane by continuous light taps on the soles of his feet. I am sure I would have welcomed those methods—any or all of them—in preference to that infernal crackling in my ears that kept up hour after hour, broken only at intervals when my torturer paused to ask me if I was ready to talk.

"Finally I seemed to lose all sense of hearing as such. Each click of the instrument was marked by a sharp pain that seemed to shoot through my skull and down every nerve in my body to my very toes. I tottered on the verge of delirium, but fought against it with all my remaining will.

"At last I must have lapsed into momentary unconsciousness. I came to again with a name on my lips. I knew, that in my half-consciousness, I had spoken aloud the name of some acquaintance, but whose I did not know, nor do I know now. And I am half crazy with the fear that I may in that instant have betrayed one of you."

He stopped again and rubbed his head slowly like a man still in a daze, his face a picture of utter misery. Fleckner and I looked at each other, and each read in the other's face an uneasy echo of Priestley's fear.

CHAPTER XVI
The Crime Trust Invokes the Law

THE rest of Priestley's story made little impression on me. I was too absorbed in speculation as to what he might have said in that moment of half-delirium. Had we been betrayed, and could we expect at any moment some insidious attack by the gang?

I gathered, half hearing, that when Priestley came to with the unrecognized name on his lips, the clicking of the telephone instrument had ceased. It must have been at about that moment that word came to the watcher above his prison-grave to release him, for he became conscious of a sweetish, suffocating vapor, evidently an anesthetic sent down through the tube mentioned by his tormentor. He lost consciousness completely this time, and did not recover it again until he had been carried in the cab almost to the point where he was let go.

His story completed, he sat back exhausted and listened apathetically to Fleckner and myself discussing our next steps. The possibility that one or more of our names, in addition to Priestley's, was in the possession of the crime trust was the most serious thing to consider.

We were keeping the crime trust principals on the screen as usual, but recent events had made them more than ever cautious, and we gleaned nothing of value as to their information and plans. Our chief dread was that Priestley had let slip the name of Professor Fleckner. In that case we could expect an attack on the laboratory at any moment. What insidious form it would take we could not imagine, and hence could not prepare very intelligently to meet it.

One thing was certain. If Fleckner had been betrayed and the secret of the telephonoscope discovered by the trust, our game was up.

"At the least," I said, "we must all stay hidden here at the laboratory. Priestley certainly can't show his face in public until we've got this bunch nipped. I advise keeping even your servants shut in on some pretext or other."

"Right!" Fleckner agreed; "and we must use extreme caution in answering both the door and telephones. I'll have Miss Stimson stand guard over those matters."

"But Miss Stimson is out!" Priestley cried in sudden alarm. "We must get her back at once. They may have her name and be after her now."

He sprang for the telephone, unmindful of his physical weakness.

Fleckner made a move as if to stop him, but immediately seemed to think better of it.

"Don't say who's calling," he warned Priestley instead. "I instructed her when I hired her to keep her employment absolutely secret."

Miss Stimson lived alone at an apartment hotel. In a moment Priestley had the desk clerk there on the phone and asked for her.

After listening to the clerk's report he hung up and turned back to us, his face even paler than before.

"They say she isn't there, and hasn't been in her room for several days."

"Then they've got her!" I exclaimed.

Priestley sank into a chair and dropped his face in his hands, too overcome to speak.

Professor Fleckner was lost in thought, but said nothing, and his masklike countenance betrayed no emotion.

"The poor girl!" I exclaimed. "They'll torture her horribly! There must be some way of rescuing her!"

"I'll give myself up in exchange," Priestley declared. "Let me at the instrument."

He went to the switchboard of the telephonoscope and threw over the control lever. Professor Fleckner watched him with a sardonic smile.

But to our bewilderment nothing happened in response to Priestley's manipulation of the levers. The screen remained blank.

Fleckner chuckled.

"It won't work, will it?" he taunted. "You see, I have noted that you boys didn't quite approve of my methods and might get rebellious. So while you slept, I changed the combination of the instrument so that no one but me can work it hereafter.

"Furthermore, I had this apartment built over some years ago when I began making secret inventions. I didn't propose to have my

ideas stolen. The doors and windows have secret electric locks, steel bars that thrust across them out of the interior of the adjacent walls, so that it's as impossible to get out as in. I've just pressed a secret button that puts those locks in operation. I've also pressed another button that put our phone out of commission and another summoning James and his able assistant. Here they are."

Into the laboratory came James, the gigantic ex-athlete whom Fleckner employed as butler and valet. With him was another man equally competent-looking, from a physical standpoint.

"James," said his employer, "some gentlemen on the outside are trying to get at our secrets or kidnap us or both. I've told you a little about it already. I've thrown all the outside locks and cut off the phone. You may break the news to the cook. He will get his regular food supplies up the delivery tube as usual and send back a written order for each day, so we won't starve. These two young gentlemen are friends of mine, but don't quite agree with me just now. Keep them under guard, especially while they are in the laboratory. They'll have access to this and their two bedrooms only. You take the day watch and John the night watch."

Then he turned to us.

"I think I understand some things a little better than you boys," he said. "I think I can guarantee that Miss Stimson will suffer no serious harm before I rescue her. I also think I can control the crime trust pretty well from now on, and I don't propose to have any misguided interference."

Priestley threw up his hands and gave in without further words, and I followed his example.

At that moment the newspaper delivery tube clicked and dropped the morning papers on the table back of us. We each picked up one and sat down to read, not expecting much of interest in the news that found its way into print. It served rather as a welcome distraction from the tension.

But on this particular morning, we found that, instead of furnishing distraction, the news bore vitally on our troubles. At last the crime trust's activities had broken into public print.

Not that the startling tales on the front pages would reveal to the uninitiated the handiwork of that evil coterie. Even I read for some distance into the first item that caught my eye before I suspected it. The heavy three-column head ran:

TWELVE RICH MEN VANISH; VICTIMS OF KIDNAPING PLOT.

In the last twenty-four hours, it seemed, reports had come to police headquarters, one after the other, of the mysterious disappearance of a dozen of the best known business men or bankers in the city. Ten of them had responded to mysterious telephone calls at their offices, hur-rying out without any explanations, and saying they would be back within an hour or so. None of them had been seen or heard of since.

The remaining two, so office associates testified, had received calls of a mysterious nature to which they had refused to respond. One of them was driving home from the theater that night when his car was stopped by a pair of masked men in a quiet spot. He had been dragged out of his car and carried off before his frightened family, who were with him, realized what was happening.

The other had been called to his door just before retiring, by a thick-set, bearded man, as the butler described him, who refused to come in. When the master failed to return after some time, the butler went to the door to find him gone. He had not been heard of since.

I read the list of the victims over twice before its significance dawned on me. I had copied the list of names on my memorandum pad in this very room less than a year ago. It was a complete catalogue of the men Fleckner had invited to witness the first exhibition of the telephonoscope on that memorable New Year's Eve.

"Why," I exclaimed, "this is the crime trust's work! They've caught every man, excepting ourselves, who knows anything at all of the existence of the telephonoscope."

"Huh?" grunted Fleckner. "Oh, you are reading the other story. I was reading the one on the right-hand side of the page."

The old man had turned deadly pale. I saw him visibly frightened for the first time.

Then, before I could turn to the account that had caused this remark, I heard a groan from Priestley. He, too, was staring at head-lines opposite the ones that had just bowled me over. I noted them now for the first time, and my own feelings were hardly less acute than that of my companions.

This is what caught my eye:

THOMAS PRIESTLEY, MULTIMILLIONAIRE, FLEES JUSTICE AFTER INDICTMENT

Accused of obtaining huge fortune by fraud, he escapes officers after thrilling auto race through city parks

------

The crime trust, defeated in its purpose to hold Priestley an illegal prisoner, had laid a clever plot and invoked the aid of the law against him.

CHAPTER XVII
Fleckner Usurps
the Crime Throne

PRIESTLEY controlled himself with difficulty while we read the two stories through. According to the second article, a cousin of Priestley's—evidently the one whose life we had saved from

the Bolshevik outlaws on that Pacific island last New Year's Eve—had just returned to civilization after long isolation in the South Seas. He had learned for the first time that Thomas Priestley held the family fortune by virtue of the signatures of the other descendants. Thereupon he had gone to the district attorney's office and declared he had never signed the release.

It was significant that he fell into the hands of Assistant District Attorney Winter, accredited member of the crime trust's inner councils. Winter investigated the alleged signature of the returned cousin on the release document, and his expert had pronounced it a forgery. Moreover, it was shown that on the date the signature was signed, December 31, 1999, the cousin was in the South Seas and the paper had been filed long before it could possibly have reached New York from there. The reader will remember that this cousin, like the other two, signed the projected shadow of the release and that the signature was actually recorded by a photographic process on real paper in New York.

The grand jury being in session, an indictment had been jammed through immediately and an order for arrest obtained. Priestley, not being found in his usual haunts and not having been seen there for several days, a general alarm had been sent out for him. A detective had seen him that noon getting into a car with a heavily veiled young woman whose identity was unknown. He had summoned help and given chase.

Then a strange thing had happened, proof of a carefully worked out conspiracy. The story went on to tell how the detectives had been foiled by a heavy cable stretched across the road.

It was a plausible tale and sensational in the extreme. It not only ruined Priestley's reputation, both by direct statements and countless cleverly put and evidently inspired innuendoes, but from a legal stand, point seemed to present a pretty clear case against him, that could be contested only by exposing the secret of the telephonoscope, which in the present circumstances would do more harm than good.

Further than that, the only persons who could testify as to the genuineness of the signature of Priestley's cousin, barring Fleckner, Priestley, and myself, had been kidnaped, so that nothing of that sort would interfere with the trust's plans. I pointed this out to Fleckner.

"And in addition to that," I went on, "if they knew enough about us to capture all the men who are in the secret, they certainly know your connection with it and will be after us at once. I only wonder they haven't been here already."

"Quite so," Fleckner agreed. "Their delay is probably caused by the necessity for keeping such moves secret. Well, we'll prove an alibi as far as this place is concerned."

"James," he directed, "tell the cook to order enough food staples sent up this morning to last about a month, together with the canned and concentrated supplies we have on hand. Then you bring a couple of trunks and a bag out here, and you and John and the cook put on your own things and get your valises. Then call up and have a big motor hack down at the door in half an hour. Tell them we want to catch the ten thirty at the Pennsylvania Station."

Priestley looked up in amazed alarm.

"You're not going to attempt to leave," he exclaimed, "and keep me locked up here alone?"

"Keep your seat, Thomas," Fleckner reassured him. "I'm going to do nothing of the sort. The management of the building and the crime trust sleuths are simply going to think they see us departing. Oh, by the way, James—also call up the superintendent and tell him we're going away for a month or so, taking a trip down through the Andes or any other remote place that sounds good to you."

A half-hour later Fleckner turned on the telephonoscope and got the front entrance of the building on the screen. The motor hack he had ordered stood waiting. Fleckner's two men brought one of the trunks in front of the screen and went through the motions of walking while the professor turned on the projector and sent their images out into the hall down the elevator and out to the hack. He held the image of the trunk in the hack, while, with another ray, he brought the images of the men back up to the laboratory to go through the motions with the other trunk.

Then all four of us carrying bags were projected in image down aboard the hack. Fleckner told the chauffeur to draw down the curtains and drive to the Pennsylvania Station. The professor kept our images and those of the trunks and bags aboard the hack all the way to the station.

"This is on my account at the livery," he said to the driver on the hack's arrival at the station. He could not, of course, satisfy the man with shadow money. "By the way, while I'm having the baggage taken in, would you mind telephoning for me? I've just time to catch the train. Call up the superintendent of my building and tell him that my attorney, Mr. Forsyth, will attend to my rent while I'm gone. I forgot to tell him. Add a dollar for yourself to my bill."

This, of course, was mere by-play to get the driver away long enough to dissolve our images without causing him undue astonishment.

All this time Fleckner had kept another ray playing about, watching for trailers of the hack, but if the trust had any emissaries watching our supposed movements we failed to catch them at it.

"Well," Fleckner said at last, "it looks as if we were all snug and could defy the trust indefinitely. If they try breaking in here illegally, they'll get an unpleasant surprise. If they try invoking the law through a permit to secure evidence, I have another sort of surprise.

"As for your case, Priestley, don't worry about it. I will arrange to have no further action taken on it until you are caught, which will be never unless I see fit. When we're good and ready, provided you make me no more trouble, we'll clear your name in such spectacular fashion that there'll be no doubt left in the public mind."

"Do you mind telling us how you expect to accomplish all these marvels?" Priestley asked rather sarcastically.

"You'll see, little by little," the professor replied imperturbably. "From now on I am the real head of the crime trust, I'm going to rule with a lightning rod. I'm going to stand it on its head. And all not without profit to myself. For the Treasure of Tantalus is mine to have and to hold."

Priestley and I remained silent. We had learned by now the unwisdom of arguing with him. There was a wild, almost mad, gleam in the old man's eyes. I wondered if the vision of too much power had unbalanced his reason. Or had we, in our desire to root the hidden criminals from society, put ourselves in the hands of a master criminal?

Priestley and I often discussed these questions cautiously between ourselves during the coming weeks when we were alone together in one of our rooms and were sure the old man was preoccupied with his screen.

And as the days went, evidence piled up that this old genius who had so enthusiastically started on the hunt for high-grade defectives, had himself developed a defective streak. I began to wonder more than ever who of us was immune from this obscure mental malady. There were times when I found myself applying tests to myself to see if I was morally normal.

All that day, after Fleckner had put his house in order for a possible siege, he sat by his desk in deep thought, now and then making notes on a pad. During that time he made no use at all of the telephonoscope. He was evidently, as we came to learn later, planning out the details of one of the most ambitious bids for power that the world has ever known, a campaign that had for its aim the subjection of society, holding its privacy for ransom.

At six o'clock that evening he sprang suddenly into action. He retired to his bedroom for a moment, and when he returned, we were amazed to see him attired in a black robe and mask like those worn in the crime trust's secret clubroom.

"I'm going to pay some of my new subjects a visit," he remarked casually as he sat down at the telephonoscope switchboard.

He then switched on the ray by a new and complicated combination

device of which we could make nothing, though we watched closely. At once the private dining-room at the Riccadona was on the screen. Then we sat and waited.

A half-hour later Judge Tanner, Dorgan and Winter entered. They removed their overcoats and sat down. They had just turned to their menu cards when Professor Fleckner arose, turned on his projector, and clapped his hands.

The trio of rascals at the little table miles away leaped to their feet in startled amazement just as the heavy draperies of one of the windows seemed to melt silently into the frames and a black-robed, masked figure stepped off the sill and stood before them.

"Pray, sit down, gentlemen. Don't be alarmed," he commanded in a good imitation of the hoarse whisper Tanner had heard so many times over the secret telephone circuit.

The three obeyed, pale and shaken.

"I am the Man Higher Up, before you in person at last," announced the apparition solemnly. "I never expected to give you a personal interview here. You remember I said to you, Judge Tanner, on election night, that I would like very much to thank you in person, but that it was not possible. You and Mr. Dorgan made it clear when you initiated Mr. Winter here that it wasn't done."

The three winced at hearing their names pronounced in this off-hand manner. They had evidently believed that the Man Higher Up was as ignorant of their identity as they were of his.

Priestley and I, standing behind the black-robed figure of the real Fleckner and peering over at his projected image on the screen, hardly dared breathe lest the slightest sound from us be likewise projected into the tense atmosphere of the little dining-room, miles away, and mar the illusion the professor was creating.

"But new conditions have arisen," the black-robed image went on, while his hearers, their first terror subsiding, stared at the blank mask in hypnotized fascination. "Somewhere in this carefully worked out organization, a leak has sprung. It has proven so mysterious and baffling that I dared not use our regular indirect methods in conducting a conference. So I am here, though you will appreciate the wisdom of my concealing my personality.

"In the first place, Judge Tanner, don't use this secret telephone circuit again. I'm afraid it's unsafe. Recent events make me think some of our telephone communications have been tapped. When I need to confer with you I'll call you on the regular telephone at your home or your chambers and simply ask: 'Has there been a decision in that last case yet?' You will simply answer that there has not and hang up.

"Then you will come immediately to this room. I'll be here. When you have orders to transmit to your helpers below, I'll see that they get there. I'm explaining to them also that they must not use the phones for organization business till this mystery has been cleared up."

Priestley and I looked at each other, unwilling admiration in our faces. At one clever stroke Fleckner had cut Chandler off from all communication with the crime trust of which he had been the head.

"Now," the apparition went on, "I've decided on a different course toward the prisoners we are holding. We'll have no executions and no more tortures. We'll keep them comfortable. Make each one think some one else has confessed and promise him immunity if he'll corroborate the confession."

"Prisoners?" Tanner asked, finding his voice for the first time. "We have only one prisoner—Gersten—and I was about to report to you tonight that we've proved him innocent and ask your permission to release him."

"Ah!" Fleckner exclaimed. "I'm glad to hear it. Release him, by all means. By prisoners I meant also Priestley. I forgot for a moment I had not yet told you my special corps has just recaptured him. So we are safe from him personally, but he has friends we must catch. By the way, Winter, let that indictment lie idle until I give the word. I may decide to have it quashed. Have you learned anything new as to the methods by which our secrets are leaking out or how Priestley escaped?"

"Not a thing," Tanner admitted. "We are still absolutely in the dark."

"Didn't Priestley make any remark under torture that could give you a clue?" pursued the pseudo crime trust chief.

Tanner looked distinctly uncomfortable, and hesitated.

"I trust you are not trying to conceal anything," Fleckner went on sharply.

"I won't conceal anything," Tanner admitted, "but first may I beg immunity from the usual punishment for having obtained forbidden knowledge? I can't believe anyhow, that what Priestley said was true."

Priestley clutched my arm convulsively. We were about to learn what my friend had revealed in his delirium, that half-remembered shouting of a name which haunted him ever since with the fear that he had betrayed one of us.

"Have no fear," Fleckner consoled Tanner. "This is an unusual occasion. We must grasp at any straw of information we can get. I'll see that all precedent is waived in this case."

"Well, then," Tanner faltered, "the young man shouted once, just as he was coming out of a semi-delirious stupor brought on by his suffering. The attendant heard him clearly, so there's no mistake. 'Mortimer Chandler, President-elect of the United States, is the real head of the crime trust,' is what he said."

CHAPTER XVIII
Chandler Springs a Surprise

PROFESSOR FLECKNER started visibly at this announcement that Priestley, in his delirium, had revealed to the members of the crime trust the carefully guarded name of their mysterious chief. Priestley and I, as well as the three uneasy figures around the table in the little dining-room, waited breathlessly for his reply.

He was not quick to make it. For some moments he stood in silence, evidently debating how he should meet this unexpected situation. At length he spoke solemnly, deliberately.

"It has been our policy neither to affirm nor to deny guesses as to the identity of any of our members, but to punish swiftly those who venture to guess. This case is different. I feel that I should set you right.

"I am troubled to know that young Priestley has learned so much as to guess rightly at the existence of our secret organization, and that we are interested in Mortimer Chandler, whom for our purposes, we have put up for President of the United States. For the rest of his delirious statement, while he was buried alive and under nerve racking torture, it's at most a very bad guess. Chandler and I are not one and the same person at all, nor does he even dream who I am. I am head of the crime trust, as our prisoner was pleased to call it. Therefore Chandler is not. That's all for now. Follow my instructions, and I'll appoint another meeting soon."

His image backed to the window. Again the draperies seemed to melt and he vanished. He threw off the projector, snatched off his black mask, and turned to us, wiping beads of sweat from his face.

"Well," he remarked with great satisfaction, "I've spiked Chandler's guns and found out what I wanted to know. The gentlemen of the crime trust haven't learned a thing about the telephonoscope, and never will, for every one who knows anything about it is safely out of their reach."

"But," Priestley protested in bewilderment, "what about Miss Stimson and the twelve men who were present at the demonstration on New Year's Eve? I thought we were satisfied they were in the power of the trust? Have they escaped?"

"You mean you were satisfied," Fleckner chuckled. "I might as well tell you about that now. They have not escaped. They were never kidnaped by the trust, for the simple reason that I took good care that they shouldn't be by kidnaping them first myself."

"What!" I exclaimed. "Do you mean to say that all this time you have known where Miss Stimson was?"

"Exactly," he agreed. "Miss Stimson never left this building that night I said I sent her home while you and Priestley slept, nor has she since. She is perfectly safe and comfortable, though rather closely confined. You see, I rent four adjoining apartments in this house. The twelve missing gentlemen are here also. Ten of them came unsuspectingly in response to my telephone invitation, of which the papers spoke; the other two dallied, so they had to be carried here by my two men, James and John, incidents which the papers also told about luridly. The safety of all of us depended on such precautions, to say nothing of the success of my future plans."

The feelings of Priestley and myself were too mixed to allow us to speak. We stared at the professor in amazed silence. Then another suggestion intruded itself in my mind.

"And the disappearance of the two-million-dollar treasure van after Chandler was scared off? Was that also engineered by you?" I asked.

"Exactly," he agreed. "When we were watching Chandler on his way to meet the treasure van, I had John and James—who, by the way, are expert aeronauts—in a swift plane of mine in my hangar on the roof of this building, ready to fly to the spot the moment Chandler revealed to us the hiding-place of the main treasure. When I saw there was no hope that Chandler or any agent of his would dare try to go back to the van after he was frightened by Miss Stimson, I decided I wouldn't let an unclaimed treasure, even a paltry two million dollars, lie around idle. So after you and Priestley were asleep, I directed the boys to fly out and retrieve the van and take it to a good hiding-place of my own, where it now lies safe."

This boasting confession, too, Priestley and I received in silence. I remember wondering at this in Priestley's case, such a sharp contrast to his usual vehement protests against Fleckner's doubtful methods, which now had passed quite beyond the doubtful stage. I was disturbed, too, by my own acquiescence.

I no longer had any doubts that Fleckner had passed into the ranks of pronounced criminal defectives. What disturbed me almost as much was the fear that Priestley and myself were to some degree infected with the germs of the same defectiveness.

Professor Fleckner was now busy with further plans. After consulting his notes and spending a few minutes in thought, he turned again to the telephonoscope control board and brought the home of Mortimer Chandler on the screen. Chandler was shown alone in his study hard at work over some reports. A hasty search about the house with the rays made it apparent that the family and his secretary were out for the evening. The servants were in their own quarters in a distant part of the house.

"A very opportune moment for visiting my predecessor on the crime trust throne and letting him know he is out of office." chuckled the professor. "Also, I may add, this is the evening in which I take over officially, the custody of the Treasures of Tantalus."

He slipped on his black mask again, got a heavy automatic pistol from the storeroom, which he held conspicuously before him, stepped in front of the screen, and threw on the projector.

CHANDLER, bent over the papers at his desk, heard a soft step and looked up to find himself face to face with the black-robed, masked image that had so startled the council of three a little while before.

The President-elect leaped to his feet, his face showing amazement and anger, rather than fright.

"Who the devil are you, and how did you get in?"

"Quiet! Stand where you are! Don't press any call-buttons! If any one finds us together you'll die first, he next!" Fleckner rapped out. "Sit down over in that chair, out of reach of push-buttons."

Chandler obeyed, as any reasonable man would. But he still showed no sign of fear. He already had himself in hand and was eyeing the apparent intruder cooly.

"That's better," the apparition went on. "Don't be alarmed. You won't suffer the slightest harm if you are reasonable, as you will be, I'm sure, when I've shown you that your life and reputation are entirely in my hands.

"Now, as to your questions. To answer the second one first; I got in by a method I shall use often from now on, for it will be necessary for us to confer frequently.

"And who am I? Well, we don't name names as a rule, in our organization, do we? I'll just keep mine to myself, as you have kept yours till now. I am, however, a member of the secret organization of which you have been the head, a member who was not afraid to use his brains and inquire into things, instead of blindly taking orders.

"I have located you, for instance, and can expose you at will if I choose. I know the machinery of the organization from A to Z. I have in my possession a complete list of the members and records of every order you have issued for a year back. Where you have allowed a leak to break out in the system which nearly wrecked it, I have found the leak, stopped it, and altered the system so that you can no longer handle it and I can.

"In short, I am the new head of the organization and have come here tonight to announce my assumption of leadership and offer to retain you as my first lieutenant, provided you are amenable to reason."

My admiration for the poise of Chandler increased as I watched him while Fleckner pronounced this remarkable mixture of truth and fiction. There was not the slightest flicker of expression in his face as he replied.

"This is very interesting!" he said, with sneering emphasis. "Some secret fraternity, I suppose, and this is the rather original and startling method of installing a new officer. I fancy you had a little too much to drink and got in the wrong house. Otherwise, I haven't the remotest notion of what you are talking about. Now, just go out quietly the way you came, and we'll overlook it this time."

Fleckner's answer was to draw a packet of photographic prints from a pocket of his robe. His counterfeit image seemed to lay them on Chandler's table, at the same time keeping the automatic ready with the other hand. He picked up the prints one by one and held them before Chandler's face.

There was a photograph of Chandler in his telephone booth followed by a close-up of the mechanism of the secret circuit and a picture of the council of three in the private room at the Riccadona, Judge Tanner at the phone taking Chandler's orders. Several views of the underground clubroom followed.

There were photos of the robbing of the trust company, showing Chandler's part in it from start to finish. There were views of the counterfeiting plant under the cotton mill at Fall River, and others showing how the bogus money reached Chandler.

It was a pretty complete and unanswerable argument. Chandler's eyes widened a little as he watched the pictured story unfold. But otherwise he showed no signs of emotion.

"Now," Fleckner announced as he slipped the prints back in his pocket, "in addition to this I have phonograph records of the conversation that went with these photographs, so there isn't much evidence lacking. I have other photos, too, if you aren't satisfied yet.

"I must be brief and get away before I am interrupted," he went on, when Chandler made no sign. "In a nutshell, the situation is this: I have learned the system by which you held your power. That alone ends your usefulness as head of the organization. Further, certain outsiders began to get a clue to your system of communication with subordinates. You know that already. That renders that system useless. I've therefore been around and established a new system, which I know and you don't. I've explained to the leaders that the old is unsafe and that they must acknowledge no more orders over it. So you are entirely cut off and helpless.

"Still further, I have built up my own secret inner circle of assistants within the organization and broken up yours, as you will learn if you try to give any more orders.

"Now, not a man but you and me know that the headship of the organization has changed. And they won't know. You will be surprised to learn, though, that one of your recent prisoners knew you by name for the head of the organization,

and under torture told it."

For the first time Chandler showed signs of alarm.

"I thought that would startle you," Fleckner laughed. "Well, don't worry as long as you obey me. I have assured them the prisoner was crazy and altogether in error. Meantime I have put the fellow where he will do no harm unless I choose. But mark me. If you are rebellious, I have only to expose you and the old machinery you controlled, and go right on with the new one I have created. Will you act as assistant and obedient adviser to me, or face disgrace and residence at Ossining Farm?"

Chandler stood in thought for some moments. He was now controlling his emotions with evident effort.

"You have me," he admitted at last. "I yield. There's nothing else to do. What do you wish first?"

"There's only one thing tonight," said Fleckner, triumph in his voice. "And that is to complete the transfer of authority by turning over the custody of the secret treasure.

Chandler was studying him curiously as he said this. His own face had become a complete mask again.

"I noticed that you had no photo of the big treasure chest. I suspect that you, with all your knowledge, know no more about the treasure's hiding-place than I."

"What do you mean?" Fleckner demanded sharply.

"I mean that you've made the

natural mistake of assuming that I was the ultimate man higher up. I was not. I was head of the working organization, it is true. But above me was the only man who knows the secret of the treasury. I haven't the remotest idea who he is or where he keeps the treasure."

TO BE CONTINUED

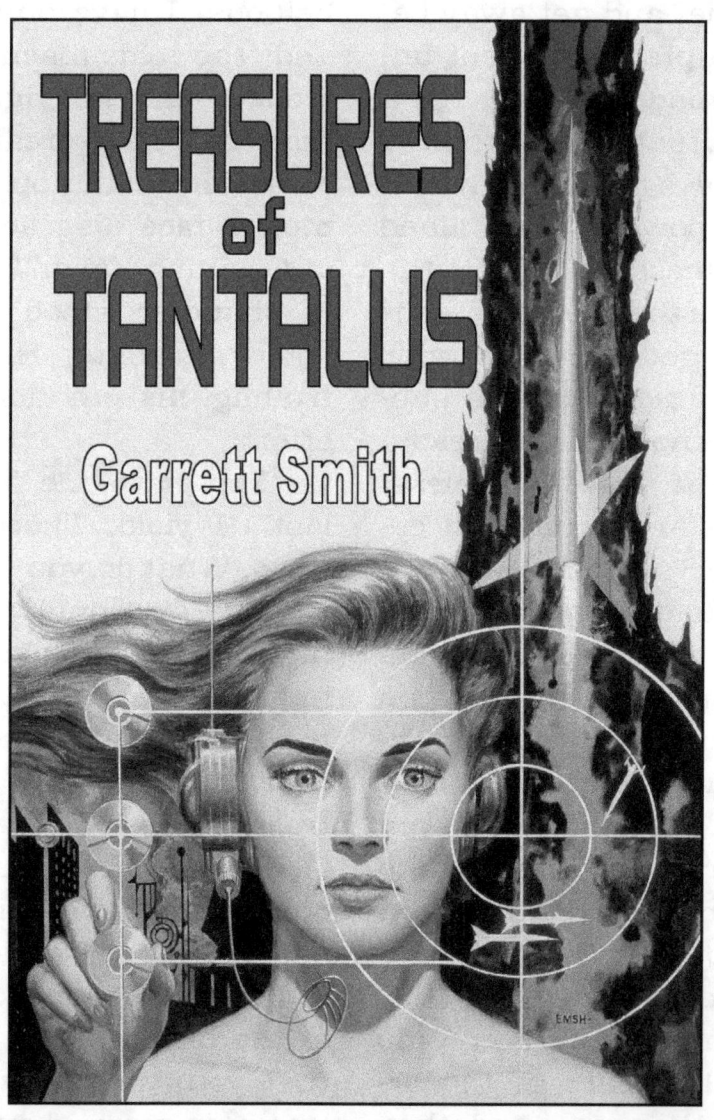

SCIENCE FICTION ADVENTURES

Writers & Artists Guidelines

Send all fiction submissions as a Word Document (.doc) file attachments via email to fortunapublications@gmail.com.

Fiction:

We are looking for Science Fiction stories in the action/adventure genre. Fiction may range from 1,000 to 40,000+ words. We pay $.001-.01/word on publication for First North American Serial Rights.

Artwork:

Submit samples (jpg) to the email address above. We are seeking detailed, realistic work. We pay $25 for full-page (8.5 x 11 inch) B&W interior illustrations and $75 for full-color cover art.

ORIGINAL FULL MAGAZINE TEXTS

The original full unedited magazine texts have been used for these books. Many of them only appear in condensed, edited, censored versions.

LLANA OF GATHOL reprints the complete four-part magazine serial from *Amazing Stories* pulp magazine and includes editorial changes made by Ray Palmer.

Once again, John Carter, Prince of Helium, Warlord of Mars, the master swordsman of two worlds, brings us a story of high adventure on the dying planet that he loves so well, Here, as of yore, he crosses swords with some of Mars' most redoubtable swordsmen.

Available from Fiction House Press
www.FictionHousePress.com

The Planet of Peril—Otis Adelbert Kline. Suddenly transported by psychic wizardry to the beautiful and mysterious planet, Venus, Robert Grandon, clubman and idler, a man who all his life had craved adventure, found it aplenty. Grandon was a fighter and fighting ability on Venus was the price of life. His adventures with savage men, ferocious beasts, gigantic reptiles, enormous blood sucking bats and other hideous animals, follow in quick succession. Then there is Vernia! This is a tale of amazing adventure.

The Swordsman of Mars—Otis Adelbert Kline. Harry Thorne, unable to find a job as a fencing master, meets Dr. Morgan who offers him the chance at adventure and excitement on the planet Mars. Thorne soon finds himself knee-deep in trouble on the planet Mars as he assumes the place of Borgen Takkor, a prince of Mars.

The Radio Man—Ralph Milne Farley. The planet Venus is many millions of miles away from Earth, but for Myles Cabot of Boston, it was too dangerously close -- for a queer radio accident transmitted the young scientist instantaneously to that mystery world -- unarmed, naked, and with no means to get home!

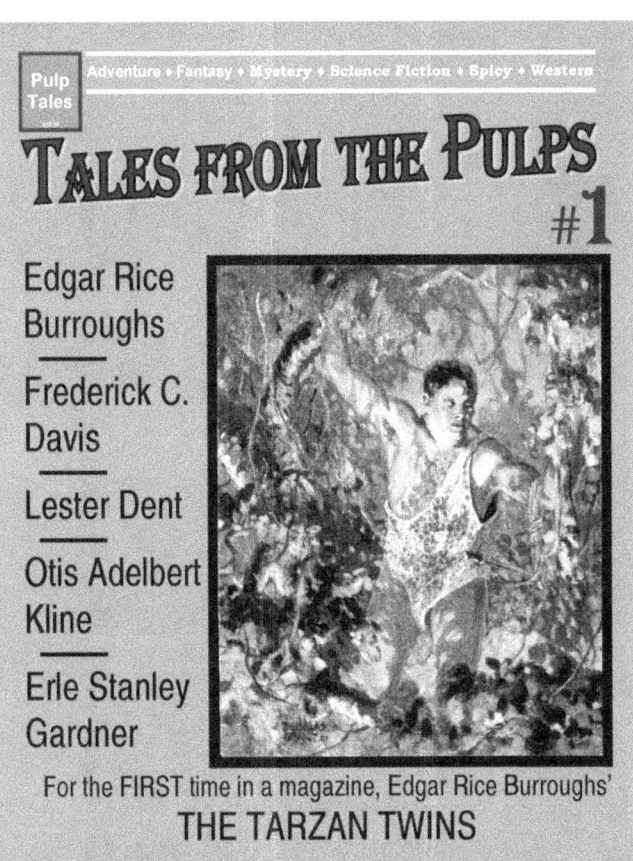
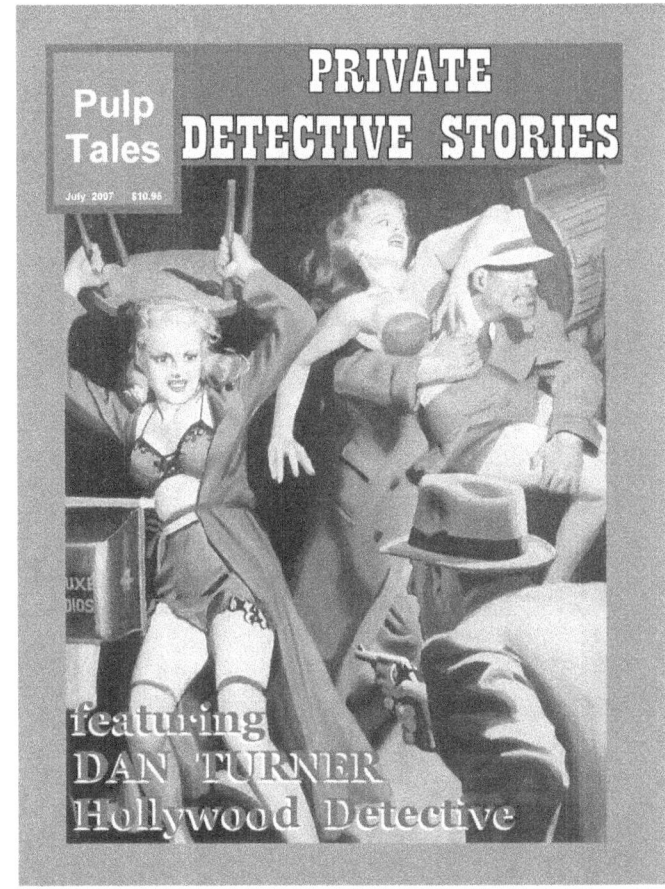
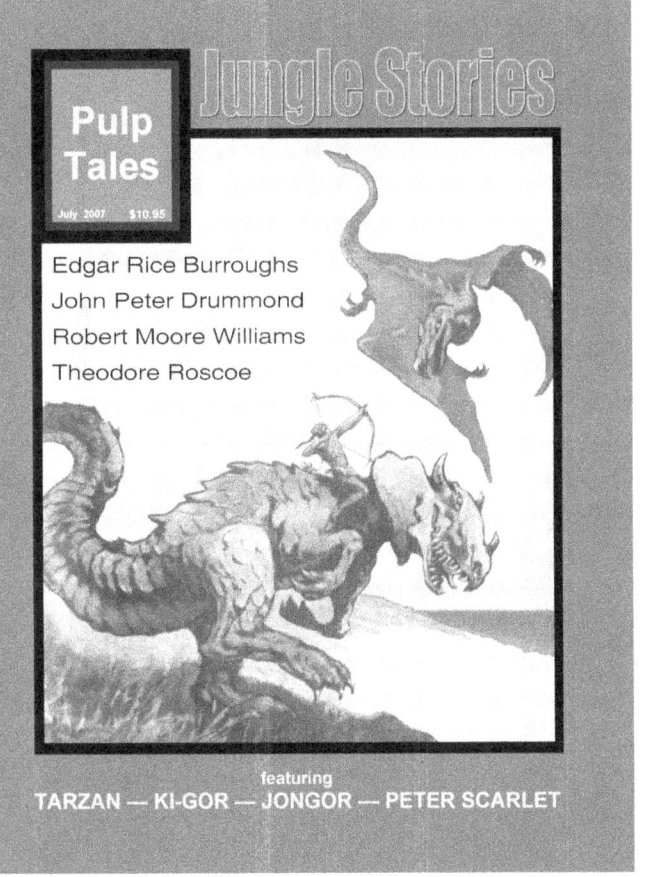

TOM CORBETT SPACE CADET

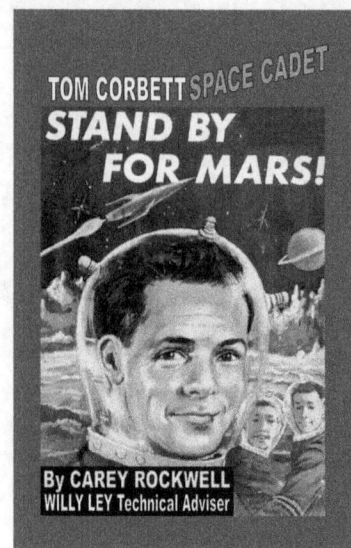

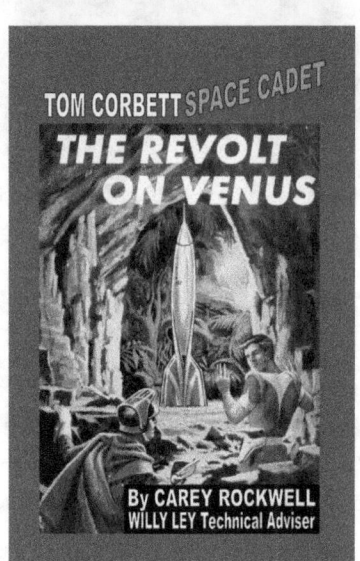

Available at www.FictionHousePress.com

www.ingramcontent.com/pod-product-compliance
Lightning Source LLC
Chambersburg PA
CBHW080817250626
47159CB00010B/3420